THEODORE ROBINS
— AND THE —
BLOOD DRAGON CURSE

LINDSEY CAMBER

This is a work of fiction. Names, characters, places, and incidents are products of the author's imagination or are used fictitiously and are not to be construed as real. Any resemblance to actual events, locations, organizations, or persons, living or dead, is entirely coincidental.

World Castle Publishing, LLC
Pensacola, Florida
Copyright © 2024 Lindsey Camber
Paperback ISBN: 9798891261525
eBook ISBN: 9798891261532
First Edition World Castle Publishing, LLC, March 11, 2024
http://www.worldcastlepublishing.com

Licensing Notes

Cover: Jeniffer Kay at Tech Flames
Editor: Karen Fuller

Table of Contents

Chapter One
Winds of Change 10

Chapter Two
Diamonds and Dragons. 27

Chapter Three
Weddings and Witches 48

Chapter Four
Captured 62

Chapter Five
Freedom Flight. 73

Chapter Six
A Great Treasure. 92

Chapter Seven
Heritage. 106

Chapter Eight
Revelation 115

Chapter Nine
Twilight. 136

Chapter Ten
A Perfect Plan 143

Chapter Eleven
The Great Escape 155

Chapter Twelve
Now We Wait 163

Chapter Thirteen
The Blood Dragon Curse 170

For Myles, Morgan, and Hallie

PROLOGUE

A dim light shone brightly against the dark of night. The soldier stared curiously as he listened to the sound of waves lapping against the beach below. The distant light across the sea was an assurance of a war that was soon to come; he and his comrades had but a fortnight to prepare, and now the time was near.

Sounds of a warhorn blasted nearby, sending a rush of shivers down his spine. The castle rustled with life as preparations began; archers lined the battlement walls, and swordsmen swarmed through the gate to place themselves on the small strip of beach that stood between the castle and the world beyond.

The soldier heard a blast from across the sea, and the single dim light soon morphed into a swarm of ten thousand. The immense fleet of ships brought about a sudden and sinking realization—they could not possibly win. He wanted to run away and to keep running until a thousand miles were placed between himself and the approaching threat, but he did not. Instead, he gripped the hilt of his sword and stood tall.

I will fight for my king to the death if I must.

He climbed down from the battlement and walked through the gate to take his place amongst the ranks. The lights burned brighter until he was able to make out the shape of several ships on the frontline.

Another horn blasted.

"Archers, nock!" A commanding officer shouted.

He and the soldiers on the beach unsheathed their swords.

When the ships made bank, hundreds of fierce warriors dropped into the water and began charging towards them. Their sheer number was frightening.

We will not win. I am going to die, he thought with despair.

Suddenly, a thundering roar sent a shock

of pain through his body. Clasping his ears in agony, the soldier looked up to see the moonlight glimmering off the scales of an enormous black dragon. The dragon momentarily passed in front of the full moon, casting the entire army into a shadow of total darkness. A cold chill ran through the soldier's body. The oncoming warriors stopped in their tracks. They gazed with horrified expressions at the mighty beast from which they knew there was no escape. A few turned and fled, but to no avail. The dragon roared once more and engulfed his victims in a surge of flames.

With newfound courage, the soldiers released a ferocious war cry, and with swords raised high, they moved forward in tandem into the battlefield of fire.

CHAPTER ONE
WINDS OF CHANGE

Morning light crept over the valley and blanketed the small village of Poplar Springs in its warmth. Unbeknownst townsfolk moved quietly throughout the village; some early risers sat on their front porches drinking coffee or tea while others shuffled purposefully down the street. No one seemed to notice the unusual subtleties that made this morning quite different from mornings past— songbirds were silent, and standing waters were motionless as mirrors. Mother birds nestled into the safety of their small homes, as did many other animals of the forest whose intuition was still intact. The winds of change blew gently through the town like a prowling lioness eager for her next meal. Still, despite these peculiarities, black smoke billowed from chimneys, and quiet chatter filled the air. What appeared to be an ordinary morning to the people of Poplar Springs, anyway, would actually come to be known as the dawn of a new era.

The sun finally peeked over the horizon and shone brightly on a house where there lived a thirteen-year-old boy named Theodore Robins.

"One hundred seventy-two, one hundred seventy-three, one hundred seventy-four, one hundred seventy-*five*!" Theo counted as he dropped the last silver coin into his pouch. Light spilled in from his bedroom window and warmed his skin, and for a moment, he watched as hundreds of tiny dust particles floated through the rays of sunlight.

It had been over five years since he and his family had a horse of their own, and now, with only twenty-five coins left to go, Theo felt as if his hard work had nearly paid off. He imagined how it must feel to gallop while riding in the saddle. He closed his eyes and tried to feel the sun on his cheeks and the wind in his hair.

"Theodore!" he heard his mother calling from the kitchen.

He tried to hold on to the image a bit longer– the horse's powerful muscles pushing him forward, the rhythmic sound of hooves beating against the ground.

"Theodore!" His mother's voice once again interrupted his thoughts.

Theo placed the pouch back under his mattress and quietly closed his bedroom door.

He found his mother, Evelyn, waiting for him in the kitchen, her long gown swaying and rippling as she moved about the kitchen. Her curly blonde hair was bound tightly in a ponytail, but a few curls had twisted their way free, making her appearance a bit distraught. The kitchen was filled with smoke and the smell of burnt meat. Theo tried his best not to cough.

"Lovely meal you've prepared, Ma."

His mother shot him a rather scornful glance before responding.

"Where have you been? Rimora's wedding is tomorrow, and I've been up half the night working on her dress. Gene and Vermilda have asked me to help with the wedding feast, and I've yet to even deliver her dress! Who knows if it will even fit!" she shouted as she desperately stirred a pot of gravy.

Rimora was Evelyn's niece and the daughter of Evelyn's sister, Janette, who had passed away several years ago from a fever. Since her death, Theo's mother had done her best to provide for and support Rimora, along with two children of her own. Rimora's grandparents, Gene and Vermilda, had already partially paid Evelyn for the wedding gown, but Evelyn was also helping in many other ways, free of cost.

"Sheilda down the street says she saw her at Gerald's twice this week ordering donuts! Can you believe it? Donuts! And two dozen of them, at that!" She began stirring faster.

"Who eats twenty-four donuts the week of their wedding? As if the job of a seamstress weren't difficult enough as it is! Who will they blame when her dress doesn't fit? Will they blame the donuts? Oh no. They won't. They'll blame the one who made the dress. That's who they'll blame." Specks of gravy started to fly from the pot now.

Theo approached his mother and placed his hand on hers. She finally ceased her vigorous whisking as he smiled and said,

"Will it help if I bring Rimora the dress? I have plans to visit Old Man Cramer today. I can stop by her house on my way."

Evelyn returned the smile and laughed as she took Theo's face in her hands.

"Theodore Robins, what would I ever do without you?"

"The house would likely burn down, that's for sure," Theo said jokingly.

Evelyn laughed and then grew serious for a moment.

"Yeah, well...I've had a lot on my mind, Theo. You know, with it being this time of year and all." She sighed. "It never seems to get any easier."

"I know, Ma."

Ten years ago today, Theo's father, Brommen Robins, died fighting in the Battle of Narwhal Bay. When the battle was over, his body was never found. Many speculations were made– some said his body had been washed away by the sea. Others thought he was imprisoned in the Queen's dungeons. Theo wasn't sure which he believed. He couldn't remember much about his father, but from stories his mother had told, he was a courageous man who loved his family dearly. His sister, Nelly, still had vague memories, but over the years, things had changed. Memories faded, and conversations about Brommen became less frequent. For Theo's mother, this time of year still posed a great challenge, but for Theo, each year, he thought of his father less. He felt guilty for not thinking of Brommen more, but what really troubled Theo was his inability to discover more about who his father was. His mother told the same stories of Brommen over and over again, but outside of her, he'd never met anyone in all of Umbridge who knew his father. It seemed as if Brommen Robins had been a very private man.

Evelyn left the kitchen and scurried into her bedroom. She soon re-emerged carrying a large garment bag with the wedding gown inside– the very one she had worked long hours on for eight weeks now. It was delicately wrapped in cloth for added protection.

"Now, Theodore, Rimora is staying with Gene and Vermilda until the wedding tomorrow." She said as she gently handed the bag to Theo.

Just then, the front door flew open, and Nelly sauntered into the kitchen singing,

"Daisies a'yellow and roses a'red,
making a colorful, young flower's bed."

Nelly continued to sing as she strolled past them. Her voice was light and ethereal, as if her words floated through the air and landed delicately on your ears. Evelyn always said even birds stopped to listen when she sang. She had been working in the garden since daybreak and was covered from head to toe in dirt.

"Nelly, where are you going?" Evelyn asked.

"To change, Ma," she replied, "gardening is dirty work. But now that the weeds are pulled and some of our taller plants have added supports, I think we'll double our harvest."

She had always seemed to have a niche for growing things. In fact, everything Nelly touched flourished at some point or another.

"Theodore has offered to deliver my gown to Rimora today," Theo's mother said, "at Gene and Vermilda's. I'm sure he could use some company."

"I don't mind coming along. I'm dying to see Rimora's reaction to the dress. You've really outdone yourself this time, Ma. She's going to love it."

Once Nelly finished washing away the dirt and grime from a morning well spent, she and Theo set out to deliver the dress. They traveled down the main thoroughfare of the village; the road was worn by the many horses, carriages, and people who had used it over the years. Finally, Theo decided to break the silence, "Nelly, can you tell me about Pa?"

"You know I don't remember much about him, Theo. I can try, though. What would you like to know?"

"Tell me about the night he died."

"Okay, let's see. I'll tell you what I remember. I was six years old at the time. He came home around sundown, and he seemed in a panic over something. He and Ma were arguing, and she kept saying, 'Just stay, Brommen. Please, just stay.' I remember her crying. He came to me, bent down and hugged me, and kissed my forehead. I remember his black, scruffy beard feeling rough against my face. 'Sleep well, Nell,' he said, and he smiled at me."

Nelly paused here and her face became

a frown.

"After that, he went into your bedroom, where you were already fast asleep in your bed. You were only a few years old at the time. He put your tiny face in his hand and just stared at you for a while. It seems as if I remember there being tears in his eyes."

Nelly stopped walking and looked at Theo. Theo stopped now as well.

"Theo…. Something about that night always felt strange to me. It seems as if he almost knew he wouldn't be coming back. I think he knew that King Baymont had no chance of defeating Carmella."

"He must have been so brave to fight, knowing he wouldn't win," Theo mumbled. "It's always…*bothered* me that he was never found. Sometimes I wonder if the rumors are true, that he is still alive, just imprisoned in Queen Carmella's dungeon."

"I know, Theo. The worst part for me is not knowing. Is he still alive? If so, where did he go? Why has he never returned? These are the questions that keep me up at night."

"Yeah, me too," Theo agreed. He thought about what she had said as they continued walking.

Could my father still be alive? Would he even recognize me? He entertained the thought for a while, and it brought him some comfort to imagine his father riding into the village, receiving looks of astonishment from the townsfolk.

Theo and Nelly finally reached the long drive that led to Old Man Cramer's place. Theo had been working tirelessly for Old Man Cramer, or as most called him, Farmer Cramer, for just over six months now. It was strenuous labor for a boy of thirteen years, but the pay was decent. Theo's main duties were assisting in harvest collection, raking stalls, chopping wood, and his personal favorite: caring for Farmer Cramer's horses.

"Why'd you say you needed to stop by Cramer's?"

"I didn't," Theo said with a smirk.

"Okay then, smarty pants. Why are we going to Cramer's?"

"He owes me one final payment," Theo declared, a broad smile spreading across his face.

"You don't mean..."

"Twenty-five coins, Nell. That's what I'm owed."

Nelly was speechless for a moment, and then a wide smile spread across her face.

"And you still have one-hundred and seventy-five in your pouch?"

"I counted just this morning to be sure."

"So it's really happening, Theo? Please don't joke with me right now. Tell me. Straightforward. Do you have enough money to buy a horse?"

"Just enough to buy that beautiful mare of Cramer's. I'm picking her up today," Theo said proudly. He took out his pouch and tossed it to Nelly.

Nelly stared at the coins, a look of bewilderment still on her face.

"Theodore Robins! You sneaky thing, you! I can't believe it!" Nelly shouted to the heavens. "We're going to have a horse!"

"Whoooooo-oooooooh!" Theo whooped loudly.

With a newfound sense of eagerness, they quickened the pace. Farmer Cramer's small home soon became visible around the bend. He was waiting for them in an old rocking chair on the front porch.

"There ya are, Theodore. I've been waitin' on ya half the mornin'," Farmer Cramer said as he shakily pushed himself to his feet.

He was an elderly man who, since his son passed away last year, had been unable to tend to the needs of his ranch. Not until Theodore came along last spring. Since then, Theo helped Farmer Cramer keep the place running.

"Alright now, come on inside, make yourselves comfortable."

"That's okay, actually, Mr. Cramer. You see, we're running an errand for my mother, and it's a bit of a timely matter, I'm afraid."

"So be it then, have it your way."

Farmer Cramer dug around in the left pocket of his overalls and removed a small leather pouch.

"Here's your payment, son. Twenty-five silver coins. Count it if ya like, but it's all there," he said and handed the pouch to Theo.

"I know you're a man of your word, Mr. Cramer. But there's really no need for me to take that from you. I'd like to buy a horse from you, sir. I've been saving up for quite some time now, and I've brought one-hundred and seventy-five coins with me. With that plus the coins in your pouch, you'll have two hundred. What do you say?"

"Huh," Farmer Cramer said as he rolled the pouch around in his hand. "And which horse will ya want?"

"Beauty, sir."

"Hmmm. Two-hundred coins, ya say. She's a spirited horse, that one. And strong, too. I'd be sorry to part with her. But I could use the extra money."

Cramer paused for a moment and extended his hand toward Theo. Theo firmly grasped it in return.

"Deal."

Theo stared out into the pasture at his horse.

My horse. He could hardly believe those words. Cramer was right to name this horse Beauty. She was an even mixture of black and white right up to her cheekbone. Her entire head past that point was solid white, and her eyes were a beautiful light blue. Her hair was black at the roots and copper on the ends.

Old Man Cramer threw in a bridle with Theo's purchase. He'd have to save more money for a saddle, but all he really needed in order to ride were the bridle and the reins. With those, he'd have full control over Beauty to steer her where he needed to go.

Theo climbed over the gate and approached Beauty. She did not run or seem afraid. She had known Theo for some time now. He placed the bridle over her head and fastened it. He placed the reins on her neck and prepared to climb onto her back, hoping she wouldn't disapprove. To Theo's surprise, she remained calm. He hoisted himself up and threw one leg over. Theo gently nudged her with his feet, and she began to walk. A smile spread across his face as he made his way back toward the gate.

"Wow, Theo. She is very beautiful," Nelly said as she stroked Beauty's neck. When she was finished, she turned and closed the gate behind them.

"She sure is," Theo replied, beaming with pride.

He took the garment bag with the wedding gown from his sister and draped it across his lap before helping Nelly onto Beauty as well.

"What's her name?" Nelly asked as they

rode.

"Cramer calls her Beauty. I think it's a fitting name."

"Beauty. A fitting name, indeed."

They had not long since left Cramer's when the sky began to darken ahead of them. The air became thick and muggy, and Theo could see lightning in the distance.

"What do you think, Nell? Is it coming this way?"

"I don't believe we can escape this storm if we try, Theo. It's too wide. Even if we turn now and run in the other direction, it'll catch up to us long before we reach home. I say we find shelter and try to wait it out."

Theo stared at the distant storm, his eyes focused on them intently.

"We should go back to Cramer's and take refuge there. We can stay until the storm passes and then continue on to Rimora's grandparents."

"That sounds like a fine plan, but Theo. . ." Nelly said as she glanced at the distant sky.

"What?" Theo replied.

"I think we should hurry."

Theo nudged Beauty with more urgency

than before. She quickened the pace to a gallop, and they held on tightly, squeezing her sides with their legs and leaning low to avoid fighting the wind. A loud pop of thunder sounded off close by. It started to rain.

"We have to go faster, Theo! We aren't going to make it!" Nelly shouted over the wind.

"Okay! Hold on!"

Nelly tightened her grip around Theo's waist as he urged Beauty to go faster. They were at a dead run now, moving as fast as Beauty's powerful legs would allow. Theo leaned closer to Beauty, his legs beginning to burn from the constant exertion. The roadside became a blur as the trees rushed past them. It started to rain harder, the raindrops stinging like ants on their skin. Farmer Cramer's drive was just ahead.

Just a little further... Almost there... Come on, Beauty. We can make it.

Suddenly, a bright flash of lightning blinded them, and an excoriating crash of thunder shook the earth with its intensity. Beauty reared up in fright, sending both Nelly and Theo to the ground below. Theo reached for something, anything to hold on to, as his arms flailed frantically in the air. He hit the ground on his back with a thud, knocking the breath from his body. He felt warm liquid gushing around him. He thought it was blood but then realized he and Nelly were both lying in a puddle of mud.

"Are you okay?" Theo asked.

He received no reply. Nelly was sitting up in the puddle, her face expressionless.

"Nelly, what's wrong? Are you hurt?"

Nelly did not speak. She lifted her arms to pull something out of the mud.

Now Theo understood.

What Nelly pulled from the muck, hardly recognizable from the thick sludge that now consumed it, was his mother's garment bag.

CHAPTER TWO
DIAMONDS AND DRAGONS

The storm passed just as quickly as it had arrived. Theo and Nelly sat quietly in the puddle of mud, their bodies still in shock from the chain of events that led to their current predicament.

"What are we going to do?" Theo asked, staring at the muddy garment bag.

"She worked so hard on this gown, Theo. She was supposed to receive her second half of payment at the wedding tomorrow."

"Well, maybe it's not entirely ruined. Take it out, and let's have a look."

Nelly carefully opened the muddy garment bag and pulled out the gown, which was still wrapped in cloth. The cloth was now soaking wet and brown in color. She removed the dress to find that it, too, was no longer white but a wet, brown blob.

Nelly and Theo both let out a sigh.

"Ma's going to be so upset," Nelly said.

Theo thought for a moment. *How can I fix this? My mother's dress… She worked so hard! If I could just buy her a new one…*

"No, she's not." Theo finally declared.

"What do you mean? Of course, she's going to be upset! She worked for weeks on this dress, and now it's ruined because of us!" Nelly kicked a rock out of frustration. Their eyes followed until it landed and rolled to the side of the road, just a few feet away from Beauty. Beauty bent down to sniff the rock and began pawing the ground. It seemed as if she were expecting the rock to be a sweet treat and was now showing her disapproval.

"She's not going to be upset," Theo said as he clasped his hands together and jumped to his feet, "because we are going to return Beauty to Farmer Cramer in exchange for my two hundred silver coins."

Nelly looked at him in astonishment.

"We are going to the Capital today. We

will find the most beautiful wedding gown Umbridge has ever seen, and we are going to deliver it to Rimora."

Nelly smiled, and Theo could see pride in her eyes.

"That's my little brother!" Nelly exclaimed as she wrapped her arms around Theo's neck and shuffled his hair with her hands.

"Hey!" Theo laughed. "Stop that!"

With that, they set out, still covered in mud, to return Beauty and visit the city of Bulmar.

Poplar Springs was on the outskirts of the mighty city of Bulmar, the capital of Umbridge, so it was commonly referred to by the people as the Capital. It was here where Queen Carmella had ruled since her victory in the Battle of Narwhal Bay when she sailed on Bulmar with a fleet of ten thousand ships and took the crown from King Baymont. The siege lasted for two days, and afterward, King Baymont was beheaded. Queen Carmella sat herself upon the throne and had ruled Umbridge ever since.

Theo and Nelly brought Beauty back to Old Man Cramer, and much to his dismay, he returned Theo's two hundred silver coins. Afterwards, they made the long trek to Bulmar. The two walked quickly so as not to waste any daylight; they hoped to deliver Rimora a dress and be home by sundown.

By midday, after an already eventful morning, they found themselves at the gates of the Capital. The castle walls seemed to extend into the heavens, and Theo wondered how anyone ever built something so incredibly colossal. The walls served to protect the Capital in the event of a siege or any possible opposition. Just inside the castle walls, on the westernmost side of Bulmar, was the Royal Palace. This was where Queen Carmella herself lived and ruled. Theo had never seen the Royal Palace before, but he heard it was protected by another set of walls that were equally as impressive as the ones he stood before now.

"Halt!" shouted a pair of guards as Theo and Nelly approached. They were wearing chain link armor and silver helms engraved with Queen Carmella's sigil, the Mourning Dove.

"What business have ye in the Capital?" one of the guards inquired.

"We intend to bring good business to

Bulmar," Theo responded in a loud, boisterous manner. "We are going to buy a beautiful wedding gown today."

The guards paused for a moment and examined Theo and Nelly's appearance. Both were dressed in cheap leather clothing that was now cracked and covered in dried mud. They looked like beggars who had not bathed in weeks. The guards stared at Theo and waited for him to state his true intentions, but when they saw that he was unwavering in his disposition, they began laughing hysterically.

"A wedding gown, you say?" A guard chuckled as he wiped a tear from his eye.

"You sure ya don't need a night's stay in the Royal Suite as well?" the other guard howled as he doubled over.

Theo suddenly tossed his leather pouch over to the guard closest to him, who caught it with a jolt. The bag was fairly heavy. The guard carefully opened it and glanced inside, the color draining from his face.

"The boy speaks truly, Edd. Look." the guard proclaimed as he handed the pouch over to his friend.

"God's almighty. There has to be at least

one hundred and fifty coins here."

"Two hundred, actually," Theo stated matter-of-factly.

"Our apologies, friends. We meant no ill will." The guard atoned as he threw the pouch back to Theo. His friend began to turn the winch, opening the portcullis and allowing them access to the city.

"Good day to you both. Please, enjoy your visit."

As Theo walked through the castle gates, he was met with the sounds of a big city. Chatter and music from a nearby trio of musicians filled the air. The streets were busy with people filing in and out of businesses. Horses and carriages traveled swiftly by. Theo felt like a small fish in a very, very large pond. Only this pond was brimmed with beautiful stone walkways, intricately designed buildings, and statues of mourning doves inlaid with gold and embellished with gems of emerald green.

"Okay, Theo. Now what?" Nelly asked as she glanced around.

Theo looked to see if Nelly felt intimidated by the Capital as well, but she showed no sign of distress. She seemed as comfortable here as she did in Poplar Springs.

"We'll start walking into the city until we find someone who can give us directions to the nearest clothing store," Theo said with forced confidence, hoping to relieve some of his nervousness.

"Right. Good plan," Nelly said.

They made their way into the city's depths, eyes wandering from one wondrous spectacle to the next. As they strolled about, a peculiar door sign caught Theo's attention. The sign itself was shaped like a dragon's head, with two horns protruding from the uppermost corners. The sign read, "Enter Ye Who Dare."

"Come on!" Theo said as he grabbed Nelly's hand, opened the door, and led her inside.

"Umm...Theo?"

"Yes?"

"This doesn't look like a dress shop," Nelly said in a loud whisper.

The room was filled with various gadgets and plants. Vines crept up the walls and clung to the ceiling. Each device Theo came across seemed more unique than the previous. He found a small glass ball that sat upon a metal brace. The ball could be lifted out of the brace, and when shaken, Theo found that the ball changed colors. It was frightfully beautiful. He carefully replaced the ball and continued walking down the hall until they reached a counter.

"Hello?" Theo called.

He received no answer.

"I think we should go," Nelly said, still whispering.

"Hello?" Theo called again, more loudly this time. Still, they heard nothing.

All at once, something flashed in the corner of Theo's eye, and he knew Nelly saw it, too, as she firmly clasped onto his arm.

"Theo. Let's go," Nelly said.

"Wait," Theo replied as he made his way toward the movement. He had barely taken a step when a large orange cat jumped onto the counter and meowed loudly at the two of them.

They both sighed in relief.

"Hi there, buddy," Nelly said as she reached out a hand toward the cat. It hissed in response and jumped off the counter, disappearing from view.

"Good grief, what's his problem,"

Nelly said as she and Theo turned around and prepared to leave.

They both gasped.

Standing behind them was an old woman whose white hair hung in wisps around her wrinkled face. She was leaning on a wooden cane that was beautifully twisted in an unnatural way. The most absurd part of her appearance, however, were her eyes, which were milky white and cloudy in appearance.

"Who goes there?" The woman shouted, her voice hoarse and shaking.

"It is I, Theodore Robins, of Poplar Springs. I am accompanied by my sister, Nelly Robins."

"Pleasure to meet you," Nelly said as she hesitantly reached out her hand toward the old woman. The woman did not acknowledge her.

"Robins, ya say… hmph. What brings ye to my shop, Theodore Robinnsss," she exaggerated his name and then laughed maniacally, "of Poplar Springs?"

Theo and Nelly eyed each other curiously.

"Umm… We were just curious, that's all. Your sign caught my attention," Theo said.

Theo slowly and quietly made his way

around the old woman, and when she did not turn her head to watch them, he realized she must be blind. Nelly made the same observation as she quietly mouthed *let's go* and pointed toward the door. Just as she was taking another step, the old woman grabbed her by the wrist and jerked her down until they were at eye level.

"Let me go!" Nelly demanded as she squirmed to free herself. The old woman did not budge.

"Yewwww!" The woman shouted menacingly as she tightened her grip. Theo could see the old woman's nails digging into Nelly's skin.

"Ow! Stop!" Nelly yelped as she once again attempted to escape the old woman's grasp.

"You are cursssssssed, my dear." The old woman laughed.

"You...can...not...escape...your... faaaaaate!" the woman said, squeezing harder and raising her voice with each word.

"Theo, help!" Nelly pleaded. He tried to pry the old woman's fingers off of her wrist, but they seemed to be made of iron.

"I ssssee...a mighty dragon...yessss...

in your future. One from which ye will not be able to escaaaape!" The old woman howled with laughter and released Nelly's arm. She and Theo bolted for the door.

The old woman's voice echoed in their ears for what seemed like hours, long after they'd finally stopped running.

"What…was…that…about?"   Nelly asked through labored breaths. They had not stopped running since their encounter with the old blind woman, and their exhausted bodies were slumped against a cold stone wall. They were deep within the city's walls now, hiding in an alley between two buildings. Theo was closer to the Royal Palace than he had ever been before.

"I…don't…know…" Theo said as he, too, struggled to catch his breath.

"Who *was* she? And what did she mean?" Nelly speculated as she stood and paced. "What was it she said…? Something about a dragon? And my fate?"

Theo pushed himself off the wall, too.

"She said you cannot escape your fate, and she sees a mighty dragon in your future. She's just a crazy old lady, Nell. That's all."

"One from which ye will not be able to escape."

"What?" Theo asked.

"One from which ye will not be able to escape. She means a dragon, Theo. A dragon from which I will not be able to escape."

"A dragon hasn't been sighted for years, Nell. They're probably all gone by now. I'm telling you, she's coo-coo. You have nothing to worry about." He insisted and smiled at her reassuringly.

"I don't know. When she grabbed me, it felt…surreal. It's as if she didn't need eyes to see straight into my soul. I felt her presence in a way that I can't explain."

Theo took a moment to digest her words. It seemed that something strange had happened, which neither of them could explain.

Dragons! What a sight that would be. I've heard many tales of the fearsome creatures, but my, what a horrifying fate – to die cowering in the presence of such a beast. He quickly pushed the thought away.

Theo and Nelly emerged from the alley and into the outskirts of the Royal Palace. Theo stopped to glance at his surroundings.

He noticed that even the people in this part of the city looked different. Women walked by wearing long, ball-gown style dresses; most had white wigs styled wildly on top of their heads and extravagant makeup painted on their faces. Many of the men had strange beards and tall hats. This, along with all of the overly cheerful smiles, made Theo feel very out of place here.

"Hey! Look there!" Nelly called out as she grabbed Theo's arm and led him to a nearby set of steps at the foot of a large building. He gazed upward in awe. This was no ordinary building; it had enormous front windows that extended sixty feet into the air. In a staggered column, on display for all to see, were dozens of wedding dresses. The dresses seemed to be on some sort of winding conveyor belt, delivering the dresses up and then back down again. Sunlight glimmered off thousands of jewels as the dresses moved, sending a moving mosaic of colors onto the stone walls. Theo and Nelly entered the establishment to find a frail old lady sitting behind a counter. She was reading a book and didn't seem to notice her new visitors. A pair of glasses sat on the end of her nose, and her hair was pulled back into a tight bun.

"Eh-hem." Theo coughed into his fist as they stood in front of the counter. She finally glanced up from behind the book.

"Oh heavens! Oh, oh, oh! Get now! Shoo! Off with you!" She said as she climbed off of her stool and waddled awkwardly around the counter in her tall heels. "Oh, oh, oh! Off now. Out!" She began shooing them towards the door.

"Hey! Wait! We just—" Nelly tried to speak but was cut off by the woman.

"Hush now. No need for that. No one wants to hear it. Beggars are not allowed in here, not under any circumstances. Out with you now."

Theo and Nelly were being pushed towards the door.

"We aren't beg—"

"Now, now, now. That's enough. Shhhhh. Out with you!"

"But, wait. Listen. We need—"

"OUUUTTTTTTT!" She pushed them backward through the doorway, slammed the door shut, and walked away with a *humph.*

They waited on the steps of the dress shop for quite some time, staring at the dresses and thinking of a way to get back inside. They had nearly given up hope when a dark-skinned man began walking up the steps. He was wearing a bright purple suit and carrying a staff. His cheeks were powdered red, and he was wearing rings with colorful gems on nearly every finger. If this man wasn't royalty, then he was very, very rich.

"Good day, young lads! Say... May I ask why, on such a marvelous day, you are sitting here on these steps with gloomy expressions?"

"Well, you see...we came into Bulmar today hoping to buy a wedding dress," Theo said.

The man raised an eyebrow at them now. "Oh really?" He said, a hint of surprise in his voice.

"Yes. Our mother is a seamstress in Poplar Springs. She made a wedding dress for a girl in our village who's getting married tomorrow, and my sister and I accidentally... sort of...well we..."

"We fell off of a horse into a puddle of mud during the storm today. Our mother's dress fell into the puddle as well. And now... It's ruined." Nelly added.

"Ahhhhh, I see. Don't look so grim, child. Why, you're on the steps of Farley's, the most well-known dress store in all of Umbridge!" The man exclaimed as he grinned and motioned toward the establishment.

"Yes, sir. We are. But we went inside and were mistaken for beggars. The lady at the desk wouldn't even give us the chance to speak," Theo mumbled grimly.

"Ah. I see," the man said. "Stand. Both of you."

Theo and Nelly stood.

"Follow me."

They followed the man to the top of the steps but stopped as he walked through the door.

"She thinks we're beggars, sir. We can't come inside," Theo explained.

"Come," the man said, extending his hand and motioning the two through the doorway. They reapproached the desk where the lady still sat, reading her book.

"Helen!" The man's voice boomed, resonating off the walls. Helen was clearly surprised as she dropped her book and nearly fell off her stool.

"Mr. Farley! Sir! What an unexpected surprise. How can I help you?" She squirmed and laughed nervously.

"These two young visitors would like to buy a wedding dress today. Please show them to our finest selection."

Helen looked at Theo and Nelly, and the corners of her mouth turned downward. "Sir, we have no business with beggars. They could not afford to buy a sheet of fabric from us, much less one of our finest dresses!"

"You will show them to our finest selection, Helen, or you will look for a job elsewhere." Helen clutched her chest as if Mr. Farley's words were arrows to her heart.

"As you wish, sir."

"And Helen?"

"Yes, Mr. Farley, sir?"

"I would have a word with you before you leave today. You will find me in my quarters." Helen's eyes grew wide, and a look of fear spread across her face. Theo couldn't help but feel oddly satisfied at the sight of her discomfort. Before he left, Mr. Farley bent down so that his eyes were level with Theo's.

"Now. You enjoy your visit at Farley's.

I think you will indeed find that it is the most magnificent dress shop in all of Umbridge. I'm certain you will find a suitable replacement dress for your mother," he said as he winked and smiled brightly.

"Sir, if I may ask. If the name of this place is Farley's, and your name is Farley, does that mean...?" Theo asked.

"Aye. It does. My name is Mistral P. Farley, and I am the proud owner of this *glorious* establishment," Mr. Farley said. Theo and Nelly both gazed at him with looks of astonishment.

"I would stay, but I'm afraid that business requires my attention elsewhere." Before standing to leave, Farley lowered his voice to a whisper and motioned to Helen. "If you have any trouble with her, let me know."

"We will, sir. Thank you." Theo and Nelly replied in unison.

Helen led them to a different section of the store, where she showed them many different dresses. It didn't take long for them to find the perfect one. "It's spectacular!" Nelly said as she felt the fabric. The dress was made of silk and was beaded with floral patterns.

"We'll take it," Theo said.

Just as Theo handed Helen his bag of silver coins in exchange for the dress, a distant shriek filled the air. He wondered if his ears had deceived him, but he saw Nelly staring at him curiously, and he knew she had heard the strange sound as well. They heard the shriek once more and quickly ran for the door.

They found that the streets were already filled with people, all of whom were on the same mission– to find the source of this peculiar noise. The shriek sounded again, but this time much louder. It seemed to be getting closer. As Theo glanced around the streets, he noticed a curious figure standing in the same alleyway they had been in earlier that day. The figure was wearing a long, black cloak. The hood was pulled up, so Theo could not make out a face. Just then, a second hooded figure appeared, followed by a third, and then a fourth, and a fifth, until six hooded figures now stood together in the alleyway. They were all wearing the same black hooded cloaks. The unusual sight momentarily distracted Theo, but the shriek sounded off again. Only it wasn't a distant shriek this time, but instead, a terrifying roar.

Theo looked into the sky, along with

everyone else in the city, to see a massive dragon fly overhead. The dragon was flying low and slow to allow onlookers to gaze upon its magnificence. It turned toward the Royal Palace, sunlight bouncing off of its black scales. The city fell silent. The only sound Theo heard was the wind moving beneath the dragon's powerful wings. The force of the motion sent strong gusts of wind onto the people below, who were shielding their faces from the massive amounts of dust that clouded the air. The dragon suddenly turned east toward the grand cathedral, which was just below the walls of the Royal Palace. Theo noticed the largest tower of the temple was beginning to ring loudly. A large iron bell within the temple's walls was tolling a lovely tune.

"Ding-dong, ding-dong, ding-dong, ding-dong, ding-dong."

Just then, black scales gleaming in the sunlight, the dragon flew upward toward the tower. It rose just above the top, flared out its wings, and sank down. Within the dragon's grasp, the once tall and mighty temple now seemed a small and fragile beam. The dragon released a stream of booming roars as a display of its ferocity. The sound of the dragon's roar and the bell's tolling combined to create an odd melody– like two extremes being merged.

Tender, yet brutal.

Elegant, yet savage.

With one final screech, the dragon disappeared behind the walls of the Royal Palace. Theo lowered his eyes, briefly glancing back towards the alleyway to find that the hooded figures were no longer there. Theo looked to Nelly, who was still staring at the sky. She slowly turned her head to meet his gaze and said, with voice trembling, "One from which ye will not be able to escape."

He didn't respond. He could not find the words. He only listened to the sound of the bell's tolling and desperately hoped she was wrong.

CHAPTER THREE
WEDDINGS AND WITCHES

A dragon..? Could this really be happening? Have dragons returned to Umbridge?

"Why is this dragon in Bulmar?" Theo finally said aloud as they approached the city gates. This was the first either of them had spoken since the incident.

Nelly paused for a while before responding.

"You know, Theo. I've been wondering the very same thing. Why did it go behind the palace walls? Why do the guards not seem alarmed? And church bells? They almost seemed to be welcoming it!"

"I agree. It was all very... odd," Theo

stated.

Theo and Nelly left the Capital to deliver the new gown to Rimora. They arrived at Gene and Vermilda's when the sun was nearly setting. They were greeted warmly at the door, and Rimora expressed her uncontrollable excitement for both the wedding and the dazzling beauty of her dress. Luckily, it fit her perfectly, and neither she nor her grandparents suspected that this dress had been made by anyone other than Evelyn.

"Won't you stay for a spell? Vermilda has made a delicious batch of buttered croissants. Come now, try one," Gene said kindly as he gestured them into the kitchen.

"Thank you. But I'm afraid we'd better get going if we are to make it home before nightfall." Theo answered.

With that, Theo and Nelly were off again. They walked mostly in silence as Theo relived that moment in his mind over and over again — the loud shrieks, the black scales shining in the sunlight, and the feel of the wind gusts brushing against his skin.

Dragon.

He repeated the word over and over

many times in his mind. He recalled the six hooded figures he saw in the alleyway and briefly considered telling Nelly but decided against it.

They finally arrived home at dusk to find their mother, Evelyn, already asleep. No doubt, she had been working hard all day to prepare for Rimora's wedding.

Nelly quietly whispered "goodnight" to Theo before disappearing down the hallway. He bid her goodnight as well, quietly entered his room, and fell onto his bed with a sigh. After some time, his thoughts of the dragon faded into hazy dreams.

Theo awoke the next morning to find his mother and Nelly loading Gene's carriage with some of the food his mother had prepared. Nelly picked a variety of fresh fruits and vegetables from the garden, cleaned them, and cut and organized them into a beautiful arrangement for the wedding feast. She was now carefully placing it into the back of the wagon.

"Good morning, Ma. Good morning, Nell," Theo said with a yawn and a stretch.

"Good morning, sleepyhead," Evelyn replied sweetly.

"I could...use a...little...help here...."
Nelly huffed as she struggled to lift the large
basket of fruit and vegetables onto the wagon.

"Oh! Coming, Nell!" Theo exclaimed and
ran to her aid. Together, they lifted the basket
into the wagon.

Theo, Evelyn, and Nelly rode with Gene
to an open clearing just outside of Poplar Springs
and spent the rest of the day in preparation.
Rimora and her soon-to-be husband, Rowen,
chose to say their vows under the branches of
a magnificent oak tree. The tree overlooked the
clearing, and behind it were rolling hills as far
as the eye could see. The wedding was set to
begin just before dusk. As the sun finally set
over the hills, the entire area was cast in shades
of orange and red. Lanterns hung from wooden
hooks that followed along each side of the aisle.

This feels...magical. Theo thought.

Theo, his sister, and his mother were
all sitting together in the third row. He heard
music and noticed a pair of musicians to the
right of the tree. The music was a signal that
the wedding ceremony had begun. One of the
musicians was a tall, slender man whom Theo
soon recognized as Gerald, the local baker. He

was accompanied by a young girl playing the harp, whom Theo assumed was his daughter. The combination of the two instruments created the sweetest melody Theo had ever heard. For a moment, he was lost in the music, unaware of all else.

"All rise for the presentation of the bride."

"Already? So soon?" Theo thought to himself. He had not told his mother about the incidents from the previous day or that the dress Rimora was wearing was not the one she made. He looked at Nelly, unable to hide the concern now emanating from his face. Her eyes met his, but, to his surprise, she seemed unbothered. She had always worked well under pressure. Theo recalled a time when they were young when Nelly had gotten stuck on a cliff. She was up there for five hours. It took seven men and eighty feet of rope to rescue her, but not once afterward did she complain. When Theo asked her why she'd been so calm, her response was, "How can I be sad when I have the most spectacular view in Poplar Springs? For a time, I was big, and the world was small."

The music grew louder. With everyone

standing, Theo struggled to glimpse Rimora enter the aisle.

Just then, the crowd gasped. Her dress sparkled like a thousand diamonds. Colors of the evening sun bounced all around her. He turned around to see his mother staring with her jaw dropped and eyes open wide. She slowly turned her head to Theo and was just about to speak when someone in front of her turned and whispered, "Evelyn. Oh my. *Brilliant* work. Brilliant! That is the most beautiful dress I have *ever* seen!" Many people nodded in agreement, looks of childlike wonder on their faces. Evelyn forced a smile and nodded her head slowly. Once they turned around again, Evelyn said in a loud whisper, "WHAT in good HEAVENS have you DONE!"

"Shhh...Ma. Don't speak so loudly! As far as anyone is concerned, this is the dress you made! No one knows differently."

"I know differently, Theodore, I know differently! Where is my dress? What is happening?!" A few people turned to glance at her as her voice grew louder.

"Ma, I will tell you when the time is right. But for now, you have to smile! Everyone is looking at you! Just smile and nod. Yes, like that. Look proud." Theo said through clenched teeth. Evelyn slowly regained her composure as she looked to see that everyone was, indeed, staring at her. It seemed that everyone wanted a glance at the person who created this glorious piece.

The remainder of the evening was filled with music, dancing, laughter, and compliments.

"Spectacular job!"

"I've never seen anything more beautiful!"

"What a lovely dress, Evelyn."

"Say, my daughter is getting married next year. Would you make her a dress as well?"

When the celebration finally ended, the three began walking home. They walked in silence for a while until a good distance had been placed between themselves and the crowd. Only now did Evelyn finally speak truly.

"Theodore Robins." She said firmly but not unkindly. "Tell me."

With that, Theo told her everything. He started with his pouch and the coins he'd been saving. He told her how he had longed for a horse and finally bought Beauty from Old Man

Cramer; he told her of the storm, the dress, the Capital, Helen, and Mr. Farley. He decided not to mention the dragon, the old blind woman, or the strange hooded figures so as not to cause any unnecessary worry. Evelyn remained silent for quite some time. Theo could see that she was focused and thinking intently about what he had said.

"Theodore, Nelly. You are both such wonderful children. You can't imagine my pride at being able to call myself your mother." She paused and wiped a tear from her eye. "But, it seems that we have both been keeping secrets from one another. I have something I'd like to tell you as well." Theo and Nelly both stopped walking and stared at her.

Mother has never kept anything from us before! Theo thought.

"What?" They said in unison, the sound of surprise apparent in both their voices.

"Walk with me, now. Listen."

Theo quickened his pace, as did Nelly, until they each walked alongside their mother.

"Where did your father work?" Evelyn asked. Theo and Nelly both glanced at her with confused expressions.

"Answer. This is important."

"He worked as an armorer in Bulmar for a man named Commander Collings," Nelly stated.

"Right. Of course! Nubert J. Collings. That's the one. Yes. Well, in the spring, when I went to Bulmar to visit Curbane's Fabric to stock up on some of my supplies, I found that they had hired a new clerk. He was an odd fellow, yapping on about the Queen and some grand announcement to be made at the Festival this year, with it being the ten-year anniversary of her accession and all. Anyways, one thing in particular that he said caught my attention; he said he, too, had worked in the armory, not for Commander Collings though, but for Commander 'Banesbone,' as he'd called him. When I corrected him, he insisted that the only Nubert J. Collings who'd lived in Bulmar was one who owned a butcher's shop over thirty years ago. Of course, I investigated further. I visited the armory right away, but only to find out that this clerk, whose name was Holder, by the way, was right. There had never been a Commander Collings, nor had any man in the armory ever heard of a Brommen Robins."

Theo only stared down, mindlessly watching his feet as he walked, and let the reality of his mother's words sink in.

"He... lied? But why?" Theo finally fretted.

"I don't understand," Nelly said, crossing her arms. "Why would he lie about that? What could he gain from it? It makes no sense."

"I agree," Evelyn said. "I nearly went mad. I had so many questions, but none of which could be answered. Why had my husband lied to me? And what was he hiding from me? I had to do something, so I decided to do the one thing I knew that might help get the answers I needed."

Theo looked up at his mother now, growing anxious for what she might say next.

"I visited a sorceress and begged for her help. I told her how desperately I needed to know who my husband had been and why he had lied to me for so long. She agreed to tell me, but only at a cost. She knew a spell that would allow a living person to briefly communicate with someone who had passed over, but the price... would have to be paid in blood."

A pit formed in Theo's stomach now.

"What did you do?" he asked.

"I agreed to pay. She retrieved a knife and cut my palm, using a skull to collect the blood. She dipped two fingers in and began painting her face. The rest was used to paint symbols on the ground where we sat. When she was finished, she began to chant. She went on like this for many minutes until suddenly, her chanting stopped, and I looked to see that her eyes were rolled into the back of her head. I was about to speak until the sorceress said,

'Curly.'"

Evelyn stopped now and looked at Theo, and then Nelly.

"Father used to call you that," Nelly uttered.

"That's right. I immediately knew that I was no longer speaking with the sorceress but my sweet, sweet Brommen."

Theo's mind was in a whirl as he struggled to comprehend her words. Evelyn continued with her story.

"'Brommen?' I asked. And the sorceress replied,

'Yes, darling.'

I couldn't believe it! I told him how much

I missed him and he only said he didn't have much time, he'd have to go soon. I asked what he had been hiding from me for so many years, and through the sorceress, he said,

'I am a member of a secret society known as Transfigure. I joined when I was a teenager.'

I was very confused, so I quickly asked, 'What is this society? Why did you have to hide it from me?'

He said that he could only say it was an important group of seven people, now six, who he had been the leader of. He said that the two of you were in danger and that I needed to take you to them right away. I begged him to tell me more, but he kept saying, 'I have to go now. I love you.' Shortly afterwards, the eyes of the sorceress came back down, and I knew that the connection was severed. I would speak to him no more."

"I can't believe this," Theo professed. "I've been holding on to the hope that he could still be alive for so long now. To know he's really dead is—"

"Is the closure we've needed, Theo," Nelly said. "I know it hurts, but it's better than not knowing. It's the answer to a question we've been asking ourselves for our entire lives."

"You're right, Nell." Theo turned to his mother. "This is insane, Ma. Not only did you speak to our dead father, but he was also a member of a secret society that he hid from us our entire lives. The questions I have."

I wish I could speak with him again, even just one last time," Nelly said as she raised her head and gazed longingly upon the stars.

They walked in silence for quite some time. Theo was just able to make out the shape of his house in the moonlight when he finally blurted, "I saw six hooded figures in an alleyway yesterday." There was a short pause before anyone answered.

"Are you sure it was six?" Evelyn asked.

"I'm sure," Theo said. "It had to be them."

"What are we going to do?" Nelly asked.

Theo thought for a while before finally answering. "Queen Carmella's annual Festival is tomorrow, and you know this one is going to be grand. Everyone in Umbridge will want to be there. If we are going to find this 'Transfigure,' now is our chance."

"Agreed," said Nelly.

"Very well, then. Tomorrow, we begin

our search," Evelyn replied. Theo followed the two inside and made his way to his bedroom, bidding both Nelly and his mother goodnight.

Theo drifted to sleep, his mind in a whirl with thoughts of dragons, his father, and hooded figures.

CHAPTER FOUR
CAPTURED

Once in view of the Capital, Theo saw many miles of carriages waiting to enter the city. The line stretched as far as his eyes could see; hundreds of people were pouring into Bulmar by the minute.

Here's one good thing about traveling on foot, Theo thought to himself. *We can easily bypass this line and make our way to the front.*

The three of them entered the city, and Theo noticed that it was bustling with life more than he had ever seen before. Hundreds of traders and salesmen lined the road, their wagons transformed into booths. Some were selling jewelry, some were selling clothing, some were selling weaponry, and a few sold odd trinkets of different sorts; most, however, were selling food. An array of aromas floated through the air, making Theo's stomach rumble. One booth in particular caught his eye.

"My… that looks *delicious*," Theo said as he eyed a rack of meat being smoked over a fire. A man was basting the meat with a thick brown sauce that smelled sweet and peppery.

"Focus, Theo. Remember what we're here for," Nelly reminded him, her voice stern and unwavering.

"Right, right. But would it really hurt just to have a taste?"

"Theodore Robins," Theo's mother scolded.

"Alright, Ma. No food. We're only looking for the hooded figures. Got it."

The three meandered through the streets, all the while keeping their eyes peeled for the six hooded figures. So far, they'd had no luck. Theo soon heard a noise that stood apart from the rest. It was a repetitive, chanting sound. Nelly must have heard it, too, because she slowly began walking toward it. Theo and Evelyn followed closely behind.

Soon enough, they found the source. It was a group of religious folk who Theo knew must be Pao Dancers.

Wow! Real Pao Dancers. I've never seen any in person before.

Pao Dancers were a group of pagans who worshiped through rhythmic chanting and body movements. Their chants and movements changed depending on which God they were worshiping. Theo had been told that the chanting, combined with the dancing, created a unique flow of energy that was pleasing to the Gods. Theo was unsure which God their current display was for, but he found the movements quite captivating.

"Theo? Theo? What are you doing? Stop that!" Nelly exclaimed.

Theo was now mimicking the Pao Dancers, moving his body in unison with theirs.

"Calm down, Nell. I just want to see if I can do it."

"Theodore! These are Pao Dancers!" Evelyn chimed in, "Their dances can have serious effects on the world and on themselves. It's nothing to play with."

"Fine, fine. You guys are never any fun,"

Theo grumbled.

Just then, a guard on a nearby balcony shouted, "Attention! Attention! All citizens must report to the court square for a royal announcement from the Queen!"

"The Queen herself? Making an announcement? Come on! We have to see this!" Theo exclaimed.

"I agree. Our best chance of finding the hooded figures will be at this gathering," Nelly added. The three made their way to the court square, along with all of the other people in Bulmar.

I hope the town square is large enough to hold this many people, Theo thought to himself.

When they finally entered the court square, which was right in front of the Royal Palace, Theo saw thousands of the Queen's soldiers. The soldiers were lined along the perimeter of the court square, leaving an opening just wide enough for twenty or so people to enter at a time. They were wearing bronze armor with the Mourning Dove sigil engraved on the chest plate. Their helmets had a strip of green feathers protruding down the center.

A trumpet sounded. Theo looked to see twenty or so members of the Queen's guard file out of the Royal Palace and onto the platform that overlooked the crowd. The trumpet stopped, and the man who was playing it now shouted,

"Kneel for the entrance of your Queen!" Everyone in the crowd bent down, so Theo did the same. In the silence, he heard a *click, click, click* of shoes as Queen Carmella walked onto the platform. He was squirming with anticipation now.

"Rise," an elegant, feminine voice stated. Theo rose to see the Queen standing center stage, with ten guards to each side of her. She was wearing a fantastic red gown that flowed down to her feet. A black cape draped over her shoulders and extended five feet behind her. Her light blonde hair fell in ringlet curls down her back, and her pasty-white face was painted extravagantly with makeup. But the most impressive piece of her wardrobe was, undoubtedly, her crown. Its golden base twisted around her head and merged in the center, where it then rose into the shape of a beautiful tree embellished with diamonds. Atop the tree sat a giant emerald in the shape of a dove. Despite the horrible stories Theo had heard of the Queen, he found her quite beautiful.

"Greetings, lovely citizens of Bulmar. I, Queen Carmella, am thrilled to have you here as my honored guests on this lovely evening." The Queen waved her hand as the people cheered. With one swift motion, she closed her fist, and the crowd fell silent.

"Today, we celebrate ten years of peace and prosperity in both Bulmar and in all of Umbridge."

"Don't listen to her!! Usurper!" A nearby boy shouted. He appeared to be in his late teenage years and was accompanied by two other boys who seemed to be around the same age. Theo could see the corner of Queen Carmella's mouth twitch, and for a moment, it seemed as if she might lose her composure, but she smiled gracefully and continued.

"Umbridge is flourishing, and the people are thriving now more than ever before."

"Lies! Don't believe her! The Queen is a liar!" Another boy chimed in. This time, Queen Carmella shot a quick glance at the guards to her right, who began to shuffle toward the commotion.

"For centuries, the people of Umbridge have lived in fear. Without a true leader to guide them, our citizens were lost. Hopeless. With crime on the rise, I have had no choice but to put certain... precautionary measures in place to assure the safety of my beloved people." The crowd remained silent as ten or so guards approached the boys and began arresting them. One of the boys attempted to strike a guard, succeeding a time or two. Then, another guard knocked the boy's head with the hilt of his sword, sending his unconscious body to the ground. The guards began leading two of the boys away from the crowd, presumably to the Queen's dungeons. The unconscious boy's body was being dragged behind.

"These measures have not come easily. But, as your Queen, it is my duty to rule justly. The people of Umbridge are so very dear to me, and I promise to always protect you all to the very best of my ability." The Queen smiled now as many in the crowd cheered.

"Therefore, I have done what no other has ever dared to do. What I'm about to say now may come as a bit of a surprise, but I encourage you, good people, do not be afraid."

Theo looked at Nelly now, and they both exchanged confused glances.

"I, Queen Carmella, have made a pact with one of the last living dragons in existence." Theo heard murmurs of surprise spread throughout the crowd. The whispers grew until they became a roar of outrage.

"Citizens of Bulmar!" Queen Carmella said as she slowly raised her arms. "Today marks the greatest day in history! For I have done what no other has dared to do!" A loud shriek sounded off in the distance. Theo immediately recognized the sound, and judging by the look on Nelly's face, he knew that she did, too.

"Fear no longer, good people! Cast aside your worries and see what power your Queen brings to this city and country!" The shrieks grew louder, and many people began to scream in terror. Queen Carmella's soldiers had already encircled the crowd and were barricading them inside the court square. Soon, the dragon was in sight. Everyone fell silent as it flew overhead. Theo noticed that the guards and the citizens both had stopped; all eyes were on the dragon now. He also realized that this was the same dragon they had seen outside of Farley's. The beast circled ahead once more before gliding downwards and, with a flap of its wings, landed to the right of Queen Carmella. Her mouth was spread into an insidious grin. The Queen's tone deepened, and she shouted loudly and with more ferocity than before.

"All hail, the mighty Jhaaaaaaak!"

Jhak roared ferociously. Theo covered his ears and fell to his knees in excruciating pain.

Ow! Ow! Please make it stop. Please make it stop!

Finally, Jhak grew silent. It still took a few moments for the muffle of sounds to gain some clarity.

"Jhak shall stand by my side and aid in my rule. To sanctify this arrangement in the eyes of Vlad, I will sacrifice one fair maiden. Jhak shall cleanse this maiden with fire in three days' time at the Temple of Vlad in Shru City," the Queen proclaimed and then motioned toward the remaining guards on the platform. "A maiden shall be chosen here and now to ratify our pact and honor the Gods with this... *glorious* contribution." Jhak roared and let out a steady stream of flames in approval.

Many men and women in the crowd began fighting the soldiers in an attempt to escape with their daughters. A large man created a hole in the formation and was motioning his family through when, suddenly, a soldier stabbed him in the chest with a spear. Theo heard a blood-curdling scream, and the soldiers quickly regained formation, trapping the people once more.

Guards began roaming the crowd and analyzing various girls as they searched for a victim. Theo noticed a guard coming their way. He grabbed Nelly's arm and began leading her away.

"Nelly! Ma! Come on! There has to be a way out of here. Avoid the guards!" They maneuvered their way through rows of people, carefully noting the positions of each guard as Theo led them toward a door near the Palace gates. It was dangerously close to Jhak, but he hoped that with all of the commotion, they would be able to slip inside. Just as they were nearing the door, Theo heard a familiar scream from behind and turned around.

"Let me go!" Nelly screamed as her feet flailed in the air.

A guard was lifting her off the ground. She frantically punched the man's arms. As Theo realized what was happening, he began attacking the man as well.

"Hey! You! Stop that!" the guard shouted. Theo's mother was screaming hysterically behind him.

"No! You let her go!" she cried as she, too, struggled to free Nelly from his grasp. Suddenly, Theo felt a sharp pain in the back of his skull. He fell to the ground and felt warm liquid rush down his face. Just before fading into darkness, his eyes fixated on a nearby rooftop. On the rooftop, hiding in the shadows and watching quietly from above, was a hooded figure.

CHAPTER FIVE
FREEDOM FLIGHT

The cold, wet stone floor pressed against Theo's cheek. He lay in a trance-like state as he listened to the sound of water dripping nearby. He finally opened his eyes to find himself in a dark room; the only light that spilled in came from a nearby lantern. After his eyes adjusted to the darkness, he pushed himself to his feet. He found that this was no ordinary room but a prison cell. The walls and floor were solid rock, and the bars of the cell were wrought iron. Theo scurried over to the bars to have a look around. He saw nothing except for rows of cells that stretched into what looked like the entrance to a hallway on either end of the corridor. He glanced into the cell across from him to find that a body was lying on the floor. Theo studied the body and realized, to his dismay, that it was his mother.

"Ma?" Theo whispered loudly.

In response, there was only silence.

"Ma?" Theo whispered again, a little more loudly this time.

Her body stirred a little.

Thank goodness. She's alive.

"Ma! Ma! Get up!" Theo pleaded.

Evelyn groaned and slowly pushed herself off of the ground. Once standing, she stumbled over to the bars.

"Theodore? Oh, my sweet boy. Are you hurt?"

"No, Ma. I'm fine. How about you?"

"I feel a bit dizzy. And my head hurts something awful. Aside from that, I'm okay," Evelyn replied reassuringly.

"We have to find a way out of here," Theo exclaimed. He analyzed the iron bars for any sign of weakness but found none. He pulled on the bars with full strength.

"We have to get out!" he yelled as he yanked once more. "Nelly needs us. She needs me! I can't be trapped in here. I have to get out!"

"Theodore, child... There will be no escape from this place," Evelyn said, her voice cracking. "We must accept our fate."

"And Nelly, too? Should Nelly accept her fate? In case you haven't noticed, Queen Carmella is going to let Jhak *burn* her, Ma!" Theo shouted.

"Theodore, I—" Evelyn was cut off as a guard entered the corridor and walked toward them.

"You!" the guard shouted. He used a long chain to hit the iron bars of Theo's cell.

"You be quiet in there! If I hear ya again, I'll take ya out and whip ya bloody!" the guard said. He chuckled loudly and turned to walk away.

"Filthy maggot," Theo said.

The guard stopped in his tracks and slowly turned around.

"What did ya just say...?"

"I said, you're a filthy maggot," Theo repeated again without hesitation.

Evelyn was watching with a horrified expression and mouthed the word *no*.

The guard walked back over to Theo's

cell.

"Say that one more time, and I'll tie ya to the whipping post, boy."

Theo looked at him in silence.

"Ha! That's what I thought, boy." The guard turned to leave once more.

Theo exchanged glances with his mother. The sorrowful look on her face almost made him change his mind, but he knew it must be done.

I have to do this. For Nelly.

"*Filthy. Stinking. Maggot,*" Theo said mockingly.

"Arrrrrrrgghhhhhh!" The guard yelled. He ran back to Theo's cell and unlocked the gate. As soon as there was enough space, Theo squeezed through the crack and bolted just out of the guard's reach.

"Hey!" the guard shouted. Theo could hear his boots pounding the floor and knew he was right on his tail.

"Run, Theodore, run!" He heard his mother shout.

Theo entered the hall on the opposite end of the corridor. As he rounded the corner, he found that the hallway was lined with many doors– none of which Theo was familiar with.

Please let me pick the right one. Please let me pick the right one! He silently pleaded.

He chose the third door to the left, only to find that it was a storage closet. The guard grabbed Theo by his left shoulder.

"Ha! Got ya now, *boy*," he growled. Without hesitation, Theo drew back his right arm, balled up his fist, and brought it down as hard as he could on the man's nose.

"Ahh!" he yelled, doubling over and holding onto his nose, which was already red with blood. Theo didn't waste a second. He quickly tried the door to the right, and it opened, leading into a large room. He ran inside and was relieved to find that the door had a locking deadbolt, which he quickly engaged. A few moments later, the guard was yelling and beating on the other side of the door. Theo heard a pause, the sound of approaching footsteps, and then the guard's voice.

"Jonath, go and alert the others. The boy is hiding in the Great Chamber. Bring the small ram."

"Aye," a raspy voice said.

Theo turned and analyzed his surroundings– the room was quite large and decorated simply. There was a long table in the center of the room, which had a beautiful marble top that's surface danced with yellowish-gold swirls. A large, stained-glass window was situated twenty or so feet above the floor and overlooked the room. The window was made of bright colors that made a rainbow on the floor and adjacent wall. Theo paused momentarily to observe the spectacle before resuming his search; he knew he must find an exit and fast. The guard would be back soon with reinforcements and tools to break through the door. The only other exit point that Theo could see, though, was the window.

There's no way I can reach that. What am I going to do? Theo thought.

Just then, he heard a commotion outside the door.

"You grab that side. No, not like that, like this. Here, strap that around your waist. There ya go. Now, on three. One. Two. Three!" It was the guard's voice– he was back.

Something crashed into the door.

"Again! One. Two. Three!"

Something crashed into the door once more, this time sending a spider web of cracks that emanated from the point of impact. A few more hits, and the guard and his friends would be in the room. Theo grabbed a chair from the table and threw it at the window, but to no avail. It would not reach. He slumped himself against the wall hopelessly.

"One. Two. Three!"

Crash.

The guards had made a small hole in the door now.

"One. Two. Three!"

Crash.

Out of nowhere, Theo heard the sound of glass shattering. He looked up to see large shards fall from the window. The giant, stained-glass window had been broken. But by whom?

The guards entered the room just as the head of a large purple creature snaked its way into the window. It had large black horns that curved upward atop its head and a long row of spikes along the length of its neck. As its head approached the guards, brightly colored folds of skin fanned out from its neck. The extension of this membrane appeared to be some sort of warning.

Is this some kind of...dragon?

It hissed viciously at the guards, who stepped backward. One courageous man, however, came forward toward the animal and raised his sword.

"Back! Back you beast! In the name of the Queen, I command you to get back!"

The creature hissed and made a loud, high-pitched squealing noise that caused Theo's hair to stand on end. When the man didn't back down, the animal released a steady stream of green gas toward him.

"Huh? What is this?" the guard's voice shook, and his legs trembled.

"No! Stop! Make it stop!" the guard screamed as the gas engulfed him.

"Help! Help me! Make it stop! Make it stop!" he shrieked as his skin began to bubble and pop. The smell of acid and burnt skin filled the room and made Theo gag. The man's remaining flesh sizzled away, and his skeleton fell to the floor– the sound of his bones echoing off the stone floor with a clatter. The dragon looked back at the remaining guards and curled its lip in a snarl. They turned and fled. Theo remained as still as possible. He hoped that if he stayed quiet, the creature wouldn't even notice him. But, to his horror, it turned its head slowly, looked right at him, and lowered the flaps around its neck. It stared at Theo curiously.

"Please. I don't wish to harm you. I don't know if you can understand me, but please just let me go," Theo pleaded to the creature. To his surprise, it retreated its snake-like head back through the window. Theo sighed in relief.

"Well, are you coming or not?" A voice called down from above.

Theo looked up to find a hooded figure staring down at him.

"What? How? I don't under—"

"You can stand there babbling if you'd like, but soon enough reinforcements will arrive, and I'd like to be gone when they do." The man's voice was deep and smooth.

"But how will I get up there..?" Theo asked.

"I'm glad you asked," the man chuckled.

He disappeared for a moment, and in his place, the creature's tail appeared as it swooped into the room and down to the floor. The long purple tail was lined with black horns.

"Well, come on. We haven't got all day," the man shouted down.

"But. What. I—"

"Climb, Theodore Robins!"

Theo hesitated for a moment. He could hear the voices of guards and the sound of marching feet. He knew they would be in the room at any moment.

"What'll it be, Theodore?" the man said again. Theo knew he had to act. Reluctantly, he approached the creature's tail and grabbed onto one of the spikes. He hung for a moment, testing to see that it would hold his weight. When it did, he began to climb. The horns felt cold and slippery in his hands. Just as he neared the top, twenty guards spilled into the room. A few archers readied their bows. Theo jumped through the window, and three arrows zipped past his head. He laid on the roof of the castle, breathing heavily.

"Now, that wasn't so bad, was it?" the man asked.

"Who *are* you?" Theo questioned. The man was still hiding his face with the hood of his cloak. Slowly, he reached for the hood and pulled it back. He was dark-skinned, with a scruffy black beard and big brown eyes. The man's appearance reminded Theo of descriptions he'd heard his mother and Nelly tell time and time again.

"Are you...my father?" Theo asked, his voice a whisper.

The man chuckled. "No, Theodore. But I knew Brommen. He was a good man."

"You knew my father?"

"Aye, Theodore. I knew him well. But we will talk more later. Right now, my only concern is to escape this nest of *rats*."

"Well, can I at least know your name?" Theo asked.

"Sure, kid. The name's Vaymond. Vaymond Robins."

Robins!

"Your name is Robins?" Theo asked.

"Aye, Theodore. We are kin."

"I didn't know I had any family," Theo said. "Wh– Why didn't my mother tell me about you before? How did you know where to find me? And why do you wear a hood? Why is this creature helping you? Can it –"

"Whoa, whoa, whoa, Theodore. Stop right there. I know you have questions, but right now, we need to be moving. We are still in danger. Adoria here – " Vaymond motioned toward the purple creature— "will see to it that we make it to safety."

"She has a name? Where are we going?"

"Listen, Theodore! My, you're as stubborn as your father."

Adoria expanded her wings and walked toward them. The castle's roof creaked beneath her massive weight. Her long neck craned, and she brought one large eye next to Theo, peering at him curiously.

So you are a dragon. Theo thought; it was easier to tell now that he could see her wings.

"Don't be afraid, Theodore. She's a friend," Vaymond said. He jumped up and grabbed one of Adoria's neck spikes, threw a leg over, and sat on her back. Vaymond reached a hand down to Theo, who stood frozen.

"No way. I can't do it," he panicked.

"Relax, Theodore."

With hands shaking, Theo grabbed Vaymond's forearm and climbed. Adoria's scales felt cold and smooth, except for the edges of her scales; those, Theodore thought, felt *very* sharp. He hoisted himself up and sat on her back, right behind Vaymond. He wrapped his arms around Vaymond, held on tightly, and buried his face into the man's back. He squeezed his eyes shut tightly. Suddenly, Adoria flapped her wings, pushed with her hind legs, and leapt into the air, carrying them into the sky.

"Ahhhhhhhh! Help! Get me down!" Theo exclaimed.

"Calm yourself, Theodore!" Vaymond shouted over the wind.

Okay. I can do this. I just have to open my eyes and breathe. Just breathe.

Theo took a few deep breaths and slowly opened his eyes. He saw Adoria's deep purple scales. The force of the wind pushed his head back, so with great difficulty and a bit of courage, he glanced around her body and looked down at the ground. Mostly, what he saw were the tops of trees, but he could make out a road as well. It was hard to pinpoint exactly where they were because the ground looked much different from above.

"Where are we going?" Theo shouted over the wind.

"What?" Vaymond said.

"I *said*, where are we going?!"

"Mount Dyer!"

Mount Dyer! I wonder if it's really as big as

people say. Theo didn't have to wait long to find out because Mount Dyer came into view within the hour. At first, it appeared just as a dark spot in the sky, but as they grew closer, Theo was able to make out the mountain in greater detail. It appeared to have no end. He could not see the top, even though he was already in the sky, and Theo thought the summit must have extended all the way into the heavens. The mountain's base was larger in diameter than the entire city of Bulmar. Adoria angled to the left, and they circled around the mountain's base. Theo heard a loud roaring sound, only not quite like the sound that dragons made. Adoria continued her flight, further circling the mountain and revealing the source of the noise: an enormous waterfall. She flew straight for it.

"Hey! What is she doing?" Theo shouted.

Vaymond did not seem to hear him.

"Vaymond!" Theo shouted, but once again, his voice was drowned by the sounds of the wind and the crashing of water below.

As Adoria neared the waterfall, she did not slow down. Theo braced for impact.

"Ahhhhhhhhhhhhhhhhh!" he screamed as she flew straight into the mountainside.

Theo felt a rush of water and then nothing but a wall of cold air. He opened his eyes to find that they had not struck the mountain but, instead, were hovering in the mouth of a large cave. Adoria landed and folded her wings. Both Theo and Vaymond leapt down. She shook and sent droplets of water onto Theo. He tried to shield himself, but it was of little success.

Finally, solid ground.

"Where are we?" Theo asked

"This, Theodore, is a dragon sanctuary. We like to refer to it as the Stronghold. The last remaining dragons in Umbridge come here to seek refuge. This is also the home of Transfigure."

"So all of the hooded figures I've been seeing live… here?" Theo asked.

"That would be correct," a female voice responded.

Theo quickly turned in the direction of the voice to find four figures emerging from the depths of the large cave. In front was a tall, slender girl with very short brown hair. Her posture was relaxed, and she walked with exaggerated confidence. To her left were a pair, a boy and a girl, who looked almost identical.

Theo knew they must be twins. Each had slick, black hair, narrow eyes, and a sharp nose. To the tall girl's right was a small boy who appeared to be much the same age as Theo. He was scrawny, with sandy blonde hair and an awkward disposition.

"Who are you?" Theo asked suspiciously.

"I am Chauncey," said the tall girl. Her voice was raspy and arrogant.

"I'm Lunell, and this is my brother, Luray," replied the girl with the slick black hair.

"Pleasure to meet you," Luray said and eloquently bowed.

Chauncey, Lunell, and Luray all turned to the small boy now.

"Go on. It's okay," Lunell whispered.

"Hi. I'm, uhh…Rickett," the boy said, looking at the ground and shuffling his feet in the dirt.

Vaymond raised his eyes at Theo now as if expecting him to say something in return.

"It's nice to meet you all. I'm Theodore Robins, but you can call me Theo."

"Wow, V. He looks so much like him," Chauncey said with a grin.

"I was thinking that, too!" Lunell

shrieked giddily.

"That he does, that he does. He's got other… similar qualities as well," Vaymond said with a chuckle. Theo looked at the five of them curiously.

"You knew my father, too?" Theo asked, directing his question to Lunell. His father had been dead for ten years, and although Chauncey appeared to be in her late twenties, Lunell, Luray, and Rickett didn't seem to be much older than he was.

"Yeah, Theo," Lunell responded. "Rickett is too young to remember since he's only fourteen, but Luray and I were eight when he passed. We remember him well."

"What you're seeing now, Theodore," Vaymond chimed in, "are the last living members of Transfigure."

"I see," Theo uttered as he observed the five of them. "And where's the other member of Transfigure?"

"What?" Lunell asked as her face became puzzled.

"Well, there are six members of Transfigure. There used to be seven until my father's death, but right now, there are only five of you here. Where's the sixth member?" Theo speculated. Chauncey's grin spread into a huge smile.

"Yeah, guys, where's the other member?" she teased.

They all turned to look at Adoria now, who had been silently observing them. Adoria looked at Vaymond, who nodded his head in approval.

With that, Adoria stood up, her massive size shaking the ground beneath Theo's feet. He watched as her body began to glow, radiating a soft, purple light.

"What's happening?" Theo asked.

No one answered.

He continued watching as her body started to vibrate forcefully. The vibrations continued until her very being dissipated into a cloud of dust. The dust began to shrink in size and then merged once more to form, to Theo's disbelief, a woman. Lunell quickly rushed over to the woman and draped a black cloak over her naked body. The woman began walking toward Theo. She was as dark-skinned as Vaymond, with long braids extending down the middle of her back. She walked with precision and grace and had an air of authority about her. Finally, she stopped as she stood in front of Theo and extended her hand.

"Pleasure to meet you," she said, her voice sweet and ethereal. "I'm Adoria."

CHAPTER SIX
A GREAT TREASURE

Theo stared at Adoria dumbfoundedly.

"But. But. You. How. I–" Theo stammered.

"You have much to learn, child," Adoria smiled and turned to Vaymond.

"We must tell him everything," she said. "He has seen too much now."

"Yes, Adoria. I agree," Vaymond replied.

"Chauncey, take Theo to get cleaned up. Once he's bathed and had a fresh change of clothes, bring him to the Great Hall. Tonight, we will feast," Vaymond said and raised his arms upward.

"Woo-hoo!" Lunell exclaimed.

"Yeah!" Luray shouted.

Rickett remained silent.

"Lunell, Luray– hunt a boar," Vaymond said. "Scour the area for whatever else you can find."

Lunell and Luray's bodies glowed softly as if in response. The glowing continued until, just as Adoria had, they dissipated into tiny specks of dust. The particles multiplied and grew, forming the shape of two dragons, and then they merged once more. Theo gasped.

"Ahhhhhhhhh!" he yelled and attempted to flee. Vaymond caught him and held on tightly.

"Shhhh, Theodore. It's alright."

Theo opened his eyes to see two enormous, red dragons spread their wings. The dragons looked nearly identical. The only difference Theo could spot was in the curvature of the horns– the dragon on the left had horns that curved elegantly upward, and the dragon on the right had horns that curved down beside the face, giving it a harsher appearance. Theo assumed that this dragon was Luray and the other Lunell. Luray padded over to the edge of the cliff, jumped through the waterfall, and disappeared from view. Lunell followed closely behind. Vaymond turned to Theo.

"And you, Theo, will be granted a great treasure: the treasure of knowledge. What you will learn tonight is a heavily guarded secret that has been passed down within our family for many generations."

Theo glared, a look of bewilderment on his face.

"Chauncey," Vaymond said, turning to face her, "take Theo to get cleaned up."

"This way, kid," Chauncey said, walking into the mouth of the cave. Theo looked up at Vaymond, who nodded. So, without great confidence, Theo followed her. They traveled deep into the cave, and the deeper they went, the more signs of civilization Theo noticed. Lanterns lined the stone walls. The sandy floor turned to bricks, and various passageways branched away from the main tunnel. The tunnel itself was enormous; it was large enough to fit even the biggest dragon.

Am I living in a dream? Theo thought to himself. The events of the last twenty-four hours were enough to make him question his sanity.

"How old is this place?" Theo finally said aloud.

"The Stronghold has been around for about one hundred years, give or take a few. The cave was discovered by Toran Robins, your great-grandfather. Since then, it has been a safe haven for all Shakers."

"Shakers?" Theo asked.

"That's what we call ourselves. All human-dragons. The name started with Justine Rosson, who was Jeyd Robin's granddaughter. She got the idea from the way that we vibrate before we transform, and the name just kind of stuck. It's a pretty good name, I think."

"Justine? Jeyd? Who are they?" Theo questioned.

"Other members of our family who could transform. They died years ago, but all dragons try to keep the memory of our ancestors alive. We've learned a lot from their history.

"When you say 'we,' are you saying…?" Theo asked.

"What? That I'm a dragon, too? Ha! Yeah, kid. I'm a Shaker."

Theo gulped.

"How do you know all of this?" Theo asked again, unable to contain his eagerness.

"What do you mean?"

"How do you know Justine is the one who came up with the name 'Shakers'?"

"Oh. We have a book. It's called the Dragon Diary. Jeyd started it, and every Shaker who has ever lived has written in it. You can find some awesome first-hand accounts of things that happened in their lives. It's cool, actually. You should check it out."

"Can I see it now?" Theo asked.

Chauncey laughed. "Not now, kid."

"Why not?"

"You'll learn more from Vaymond at the feast," she replied curtly. Theo took that as the end of their conversation. She led him into a smaller passage to their right. Eventually, the passage led to a wooden door. She opened it, revealing a large room. In the back of the room, steaming with warmth, was a pool.

"Here ya go, kid. I'll leave you to it. You'll find an extra change of clothes outside the door when you're done. I'll be waiting for you at the end of the tunnel."

And with that, Chauncey carefully closed the door, leaving him alone.

Theo undressed and walked over to the pool. The floor tilted downward, and the pool's edge was very shallow. Theo could tell the pool was deepest farther towards the wall, though he was unsure how deep it actually went. He carefully dipped his big toe in the water to test the temperature.

Just right. He thought to himself. He slowly submerged himself; the water was steamy and warm—warm enough to make his skin burn slightly but not enough to cause pain. He sat in the pool until the water was up to his neck and then sighed. It was a comfort he happily welcomed. Theo had not properly bathed in a few days– dried blood was still crusted on the back of his neck and in his hair where Queen Carmella's guard had hit him. At the edge of the pool, he found a square-shaped rock with a sandy texture, which he assumed was used for scrubbing. He happily washed away the dirt and dried blood that had accumulated over the last couple of days. Finally, in the stillness of that moment, his thoughts turned to his mother and Nelly.

Ma, Nell…

Theo pictured his mother alone in a cold dungeon. He imagined Nelly bound in chains in some hidden room within the Queen's palace.

With that, he began to sob.

Why is this happening? My family, my life… It's all gone. I will never be able to save them. Theo grieved for a short while as he imagined Nelly's fate: being sacrificed to Jhak.

What will they do with Ma? What reason would they have to keep her alive?

He quickly pushed both thoughts from his mind, and his sorrow slowly began to transform. He felt a sudden, burning desire to save his family, and soon, his sadness turned to rage. He was angry at himself for going to the Festival, angry at the guard who took Nelly, and angry at Transfigure for not preventing this. Most of all, he was angry at Queen Carmella.

I will not sit and sulk. I will not pity myself for an unfortunate situation. I will save my sister. I will save my mother, Theo thought to himself as his expression turned cold. *And I will kill the Queen.*

Theo finished his bath and put on the clothes that Chauncey left outside the door. He made his way down the tunnel and found Chauncey casually leaning against the wall, chewing on a twig.

"Took long enough, kid. Are you ready?"

"Ready for what?" Theo asked.

"Ready for the feast!" Chauncey replied with a smirk.

Together, they walked further down the main tunnel until it opened up into a large room. In the middle of the room was a long table with five chairs on either side and two on each end. Lunell, Luray, and Rickett sat on one side, and Adoria on the other. Vaymond was seated at the very end. Chauncey and Theo made their way to the table and sat on either side of Adoria. The table, to Theo's amazement, was filled with a variety of delicacies. There were roasted rabbits, bowls of stew, bread, and many fruits. The most impressive part, though, was the centerpiece: a large boar that had been roasted, head and all. It sat in the middle of the table on a bed of lettuce with an apple in its mouth.

"A boar like this should take hours to cook," Theo said inquisitively. "And I've only been gone with Chauncey for maybe an hour. How did you cook it so fast?"

"You'd be surprised what you can do with dragon fire," Luray replied.

The look of bafflement on Theo's face made the entire table laugh.

"A toast!" Vaymond shouted as he raised his glass into the air. "To our good health, to our friendship, and to Theodore, son of Brommen Robins!"

"To Theodore!" Everyone shouted, except for Rickett.

Theo squirmed uncomfortably in his seat.

Vaymond began carving pieces of meat from the boar. He placed a fat, juicy slice on Theo's plate, and he eyed it hungrily. He hadn't had a proper meal in quite some time.

I can't believe I'm about to eat something that was cooked with dragon fire, Theo thought. He took a big bite, and the tender meat melted in his mouth. He savored the charred flavor.

The seven of them sat around the table in silence; the only sound was the clinking of plates and the ripping of flesh as they tore into the boar. Finally, when they had eaten down to the bones, and their bellies were full, Vaymond began to speak:

"Approximately one hundred and fifty years ago," he started– he was leaning against his chair, his boots crossed on the table, and his hands interlocked behind his head. He appeared to be rather relaxed, Theodore thought.

"There lived a man named Jaxton Robins. Jaxton married a woman named Brenhilda, and together, they had two children: Jeyd and Kalira Robins. At the time, wild dragons roamed the earth, *but* they were on the verge of extinction. It's said that only three wild dragons lived during this time." Vaymond paused now coughed into a cloth before continuing:

"One unfortunate day, while Jaxton was at work, a dragon flew over their home and torched it, burning it to the ground, with his beloved Brenhilda inside. Luckily, their children had been outside playing in the woods and were not harmed. When Jaxton learned of his wife's tragic death, he was mad with rage. He sought out a witch by the name of Agatha and begged to be turned into a dragon himself so he could seek revenge. Agatha warned of the dangers of such magic; one misplaced word, and the spell could have a variety of…unintended effects. Despite her warnings, Jaxton demanded that she transform him. The witch complied, and afterward, nothing happened. Jaxton thought the spell had been unsuccessful. He went home and grieved for his wife. They were unable to give her a proper burial, as her body had been turned to ash. They did, however, have a ceremony in her honor.

"Eventually, for Jaxton, the years resolved his anger. Time usually has a way of healing even the deepest of wounds. When Jaxton became old and gray, and his children now had children of their own, he found, to his horror, that the witch's spell had indeed worked. One day, he and his son, Jeyd, were fishing on the river for trout when a grizzly came out of the forest. The bear approached them, and Jaxton thought for sure that the two would be mauled to death. His son, to his surprise, started to emit a soft light. His body shook violently and then became a cloud of dust that grew into a mighty, maroon-colored dragon. It is said that his scales were deep red, like the color of blood. Jeyd killed the grizzly and was trapped in his dragon form for quite some time before he was able to control the transformations. From then on, different people from each generation of the Robins family were cursed to become dragons themselves. We don't know when, how, or *who* it's going to happen to, but eventually, it does. There's normally some…*emotional* turmoil going on inside a person when they become a dragon for the first time. There's always a grand, or not so grand, story behind it."

There was a long pause before anyone spoke. Finally, Theo broke the silence.

"So..." Theo stammered as he struggled to find words. "Each of you is able to transform into a dragon?"

"Yes," Vaymond confirmed.

"I wouldn't believe you had I not seen the transformations with my own eyes..." Theo muttered, and his voice trailed off. "This curse, does it have a name?"

"Well, yes, I guess it does. Over the years, there's been one to stick around. We call it the Blood Dragon Curse."

"The Blood Dragon Curse..." Theo repeated. He rolled a fork between his fingers. "And we are all related to this...Jaxton Robins?" he asked.

"Yes, Theodore. In fact, Jaxton was your great-great-great grandfather."

Theo gulped loudly.

"Does this mean I could possibly turn into a dragon someday?" he asked shakily.

"Aye, Theodore. Whether it will be you

or your sister, I cannot say. But one of you is sure to be a dragon. It's rare for two siblings to both be dragons unless they are identical twins. Take Lunell and Luray, for example."

"Yeah, Pops. Twins run in the family, too," Luray added.

"Pops? Is Vaymond your father?" Theo interrupted.

"Yes. Lunell and Luray are my children," Vaymond said.

"Let me get this straight," Theo started. "All of you are dragons. All of us are related. You are all members of Transfigure, and my father was a member of Transfigure. Was he a dragon, too, then?"

"Aye, Theodore. That he was," said Vaymond.

My father, a dragon! Theo longed to meet his father now more than ever.

"He was a mighty dragon," Vaymond continued, "and very fearsome. We were all devastated by his death." Theo could sense the sadness in his voice.

"My mother says he fought in the Battle of Narwhal Bay, but his body was never found," Theo stated.

"That's because he died in his dragon form, Theodore. In fact, he was killed by another dragon. A dragon named Jhak."

Theo stared at Vaymond with wide eyes.

"That's the dragon Queen Carmella has made a pact with! The same black dragon my sister is being sacrificed to in two days!" Theo exclaimed.

"That's correct, Theodore. Jhak is a former member of Transfigure. And… he was Brommen's brother. His twin brother, at that."

"So then Nelly is being sacrificed to…"

"Aye, Theodore. Your uncle."

CHAPTER SEVEN
HERITAGE

"How is this possible?" Theo asked incredulously. "My mother never mentioned he had family outside of us, much less a twin brother! Does she even know?"

"Your father kept many secrets, Theodore. He told no one of the transformations or of his relatives, not even your mother. But know this– all that he did, he did to protect you and your sister. He knew that someday, this great power would attract the attention of people who wished to destroy it. He thought that by keeping the three of you in the dark, he was also keeping you safe. He may have put you in an odd predicament by doing so, but he did it out of love," Vaymond said.

"So you've known me all my life, another member of the Robins family, and never tried to make contact?" Theo asked.

"Aye. It was your father's wish, Theodore, however troubling it was," Vaymond sighed.

There was a long pause. Finally, Theo spoke. "Vaymond, you said there's a grand story behind everyone's first transformation. What's yours?"

"My what?"

"Your story."

"Oh," Vaymond said. He sat upright in his chair, propped his elbows on the table, and pulled a pipe from within the pocket of his robe. He stuffed it full of something– Theo couldn't tell what, but it reminded him of mulch– and held the pipe to his mouth. Then, to Theo's astonishment, he blew a steady stream of flames from his mouth, and the mulch-stuff caught fire. He puffed a few times, drew a deep breath, and exhaled.

"Well, to begin, I must tell you a little history. The story won't have much meaning without some background knowledge." He took another puff of his pipe. "I grew up at

Hutmans, a little village southeast of the Nebo Mountains, with my mother, Justine, and my father, Halderman– or 'Hal,' as most folks called him. My mother disappeared frequently and for extended periods of time, and so my father and I were together a great deal. We were close, me and my Pops. In fact, I went to work with him every day. He was a fisherman; Hutmans is off the coast of the Great Sea, so Pops used that to his advantage. He made his money from the ocean and got his food from it, too. We caught a vast variety of fish back then. Wahoos were pretty common, and so were bluefish and clams. We caught Snapper on occasion, and *man,* was that a treat." Vaymond smiled. "We were fishing that day like we did most days. We were a few miles offshore, which was a measly distance for us. I felt a tug on my line, so I gave the rod a quick jerk to set the hook and then started to reel. I didn't feel a lot of pressure at first, but it wasn't long before there was so much that I could barely hold onto the rod. I knew I'd caught something big, and I was excited. I fought against it for two solid hours before I got it up to the boat." Vaymond stopped and took a few long puffs from his pipe.

"What was it?" Theo asked.

"It was *Anola*," Vaymond said. His tone was flat, and his face expressionless.

"What's that?"

"It's a sea-serpent the length of a thirty-foot sailboat. It has fins on its head and torso to help it swim, and it is very, *very* fast. It has two rows of razor-sharp teeth and a head the size of a small wagon. The fact that I got it to the boat at all that day was a miracle."

"What did you do?"

"I cut the line. This *Anola* was tired, but I knew it was deadly. I didn't want to stick around when it regained its strength. Sea serpents such as this were rare and known to eat a man whole. I cut the line and prayed it wouldn't catch up to us."

"Did it?" Theo asked eagerly.

"Aye. It did."

"What happened?"

"Pops saw it first– the *Anola* speeding through the water at us. He grabbed his spear just as the *Anola's* head came over the side of the boat. It snapped at him, and he stabbed at it, neither of them landing their blows. The boat rocked under the *Anola's* weight, and Pops fell.

The serpent grabbed him by the leg and began dragging him out of the boat. Pops thrashed and hit and jerked, but the *Anola*'s jaws were locked on hard. I knew my father was going to die right there in front of me, and of course, I felt responsible since *I* was the one who brought this creature to the boat. I couldn't take it. I looked at the *Anola,* and an anger rose inside of me like I'd never known before. I felt electrified and powerful, and it felt like the anger exploded, and when the explosion calmed, I was no longer my same self, but I was–"

"A dragon," Theo whispered.

"That's right," Vaymond said. "A dragon."

"Could you save him?" Theo asked.

"I tried. When I transformed, I destroyed our boat. I killed the *Anola* with a quick snap at its neck, but my father's leg was injured badly. I swam with him on my back, but he was bleeding too much. He died before we made it back to shore."

"I'm sorry," Theo whispered.

"It's quite alright, Theodore," Vaymond chuckled. "That was a long time ago, and time has a way of helping you accept and heal even the deepest of wounds."

"I see," Theo said. "Well, if we are all family, I would like to know how we are related."

"Of course. I expected no less," Vaymond responded with a smile. "Follow me."

Vaymond bid the others farewell and led Theo back to the tunnel. Theo followed until he reached a room with a large circular door, which Vaymond quietly rolled out of the way, revealing a room full of scrolls.

"What are these?" Theo asked as he carefully touched a stack of scrolls that sat on a nearby shelf.

"Various pieces of information. Maps, mostly. Our ancestors have flown to the farthest corners of the world and charted the territories they discovered."

"Wow," Theo whispered, a look of wonder on his face.

Vaymond walked to a large wooden podium in the center of the room. On top of the podium was a large, black book bound in leather and secured with a lock. Vaymond pulled a necklace from the collar of his shirt, which was previously hidden before now, revealing a key.

He used the key to unlock the book and opened it carefully.

"The dragon diary?" Theo asked as he approached the podium to take a closer look.

"Yes," Vaymond replied and raised an eyebrow. "How did you know?"

"I can be resourceful," Theo smirked.

Vaymond laughed. "My, you are your father's child." Theo watched as Vaymond flipped through the pages.

"What are you looking for?" he asked.

"Ah, here it is," Vaymond muttered and stopped.

"Here's what?" Theo asked.

"Our family tree. Have a look."

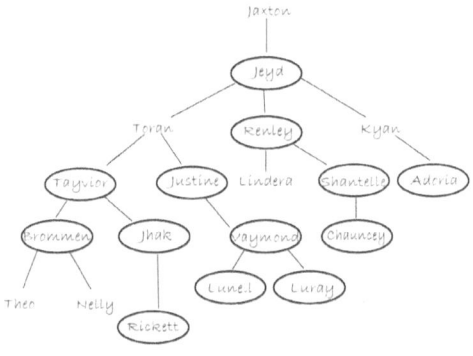

"This is incredible," Theo said as he ran his fingers over the page and inspected the diagram.

"I'm guessing the circled names are the Shakers?" Theo speculated.

"That's correct," Vaymond confirmed.

"So it started with Jeyd, and he had a son named Kyan, who was Adoria's father. Adoria has no children," Theo observed as he followed the lineage.

"Mhm," Vaymond mumbled, watching quietly.

"Renley had Shantelle, who had Chauncey, making Chauncey and Adoria first—"

"Second," Vaymond interrupted.

"Right, second cousins. Toran had Tayvior and Justine, and since their names are both circled, I'm guessing that means they were..." Theo paused as he looked up at Vaymond for confirmation.

"Identical twins, yes."

"Justine was your mother, and there's Lunell and Luray. Tayvior had my dad, which means he was my grandfather," Theo smiled.

"Correct," Vaymond uttered.

"There's Jhak, my father's identical brother, and then he had…" Theo stopped now and looked up at Vaymond, eyes wide with surprise.

"That's right," Vaymond stated and met Theo's gaze.

"Rickett."

CHAPTER EIGHT
REVELATION

After discovering his heritage and gaining an insight into his newfound family, Theo followed Vaymond to his chambers within the vast network of the cave.

"This is where you will sleep, Theodore," Vaymond said.

His room was small; a warm light from a lantern cast tall shadows on the walls. He felt safe here— no one could possibly reach him unless they were a Shaker, and all Shakers were already here except for one.

I can't believe Jhak is my uncle, Theo thought to himself as he climbed into bed and stared at the swirling designs on the ceiling.

And Rickett…

He closed his eyes and, in a matter of minutes, fell fast asleep. It wasn't long before a dream began to emerge from the dark corners of his consciousness.

A man was standing on a rock cliff, staring into the sky. Theo followed the man's gaze until he saw a strange light high in the clouds. It disappeared momentarily, only to return, but brighter this time. He looked back to the man, who was still watching intently. The light disappeared once more, and when it returned again, Theo immediately recognized what it was: fire. A large black dragon flew over the sea below, blasting ships with its flame. Suddenly, a spear caught the dragon in its chest, and it began spiraling toward the ground. Just before it hit the water, Theo heard a loud howl travel across the ravine. He looked to see the man on the cliff had fallen to his knees and was crying out in agony.

Theo awoke with a start. He was unsure of the time— in the cave, it was hard to gauge without any sunlight to use as a reference. He climbed out of bed and made his way back toward the main tunnel. When he could find no one, he walked toward the mouth of the cave. He knew he was traveling in the right direction when the thundering roar of the waterfall echoed off the cave walls. Finally, he saw sunlight; it was a sight he welcomed. He jogged now, and as he rounded the corner, he was met by a wall of mist. The mouth of the cave had a petrichor smell that felt light and fresh. Theo took a deep breath, filling his lungs with the cool, refreshing morning air. Glancing through the mist, his eyes searched until he found the shape of a small figure sitting on the edge of the cliff. He walked forward and, to his surprise, saw Rickett dangling his feet over the mile-high ravine.

"Hello, Rickett," Theo said nervously.

Rickett glanced up with wide eyes. He looked down toward the bottom of the ravine and muttered something in response. Theo decided not to reveal his knowledge of Rickett being Jhak's son.

"Where are all the others?" Theo asked.

"They left this morning," Rickett replied, still staring into the abyss.

"Left for where?"

"They're flying north to stay at Warren's Hollow for the night. They'll be headed to Shru City on the 'morrow."

"They mean to save my sister," Theo said with sudden realization.

"They do."

"We have to help them!" Theo exclaimed.

"We can't," Rickett replied. He still hadn't lifted his head.

"What do you mean we can't?!" Theo asked, a little more loudly than he had intended.

Slowly, Rickett turned his head to face Theo's.

"They intend to save your sister and kill Jhak. We can't go because you would likely get hurt or worse," Rickett said. His eyebrows scrunched together.

"Is there something else?" Theo asked.

"I'm to stay behind with you so you're kept safe. Vaymond said so. Plus, I'm the smallest dragon and would be of the least help," Rickett responded, turning his head to stare back down the ravine.

"I see," Theo replied gently. "Well, Rickett, the way I see it, we can either hide here in this cave or we can catch up with the others. I'm sure we could be of some use. Vaymond won't mind, and we'll tell him it was my idea."

"Really?" Rickett asked.

Theo nodded.

"I don't know... He might be angry if I don't follow his orders. Even if it is your idea," Rickett said.

"Come on, Rickett. Please. This is my sister we're talking about. You're a dragon, aren't you? You could be the difference between life and death! If Queen Carmella thinks the whole of Transfigure will be there to stop her, which I'm sure she does, then they won't only be fighting Jhak, they'll be fighting the Queen's entire army, Rickett! They'll never be able to do it without our help."

"I guess you're right," Rickett said and pushed himself to his feet. "We should help."

"That's the spirit!" Theo exclaimed.

"We'll meet them at Warren's Hollow tonight, and in the morning, we'll go with them to Shru City," Rickett said, and his body began to emit a bluish light. Theo had seen this enough times now to know that Rickett was about to transform. Theo backed away and watched as Rickett's eyes turned a bright blue, and his very skin started to shake. Finally, just as Theo expected, Rickett dissipated into a cloud that grew until it was twenty feet into the air. The particles began to take on a new form, and when they merged once more, Rickett was no longer a small boy but a medium-sized dragon. His navy blue scales shined brightly, and his horns jutted backward on top of his head and rose to a steep point. His rubbery wings were folded on his back, and he swung his large head around to look Theo in the eyes.

"Is it really you in there, Rickett?" Theo asked, reaching out his hand to touch Rickett on the jaw.

Rickett bent down, and Theo knew this gesture was an invitation. He jumped and grabbed onto one of Rickett's neck spikes to use as leverage before hoisting himself up. He sat right in the fold of Rickett's neck, still holding onto the neck spike in front of him for support.

Rickett stood, and Theo suddenly rocked back and forth, struggling to keep his balance. He gripped the spike more firmly and tried to hold on with his legs as well. Rickett looked back at Theo with a curious look in his large, blue eyes. Theo knew what he was asking.

For Nelly.

"Alright, Rickett. I'm ready," Theo said loudly, hoping to sound more convincing than he felt.

With that, Rickett unfolded his large wings and crouched in preparation to leap off the cliff. Theo braced himself; passing seconds felt like minutes.

Finally, Rickett jumped, and it took all of Theo's strength to hold on. Water momentarily rushed down on him, and then, there was silence. Theo hadn't realized how loud the crashing water had been when it was echoing off the cave's walls, but now that they were in the open air, the silence was a welcomed relief. Rickett strained as he carried the two of them high into the sky — high enough so that people on the ground would only assume they were a bird. At this height, Rickett finally ceased his climb and began to glide through the clouds. From here, Theo thought the world seemed rather peaceful.

It's so quiet here. And empty.

They flew north together until dusk. The flight was long and tiresome, especially for Rickett. He finally aimed for a small clearing just east of Warren's Hollow. He landed with a thud and then slumped over, breathing raggedly. Theo jumped down and buckled at the knees when his feet met solid ground; thankfully, he caught himself before face-planting in the dirt.

When he looked up, Theo gaped in awe. These trees were the largest trees he had ever seen in his life.

I didn't even know trees could grow this large! This is incredible, he thought to himself. Sounds of forest noises filled the air: birds chirped, squirrels scurried in treetops, and leaves rustled in the gentle breeze. Some time passed as Theo and Rickett rested their bodies and let their muscles recover.

"You stay here, Rickett. I'll go into Warren's Hollow and find the others."

Rickett nodded his large, blue head in approval. Theo ran off into the forest. He'd seen Warren's Hollow before they landed and made a mental note of its location in relevance to the clearing. He knew that he'd reach the town within an hour if he traveled west. As he walked, he thought of Nelly.

Tomorrow is the day Nell is to be sacrificed. I hope we can save her, he thought solemnly. He pushed the thought away. It wasn't long before the light of Warren's Hollow shone through the tall trees. Warren's Hollow was a small town nestled deep within the heart of the Nebo mountains. Hidden within a redwood forest and surrounded by large mountains, Warren's Hollow was the home of nearly three thousand people. A small river ran around the town's outer edge, serving as a barrier from outside threats, such as bears, wolves, or bandits. The only way into Warren's Hollow was to cross over the river over a bridge and pass through the wooden gates, which were guarded during the day and locked at night. Luckily for Theo, he crossed over the bridge just as the gates were beginning to close.

"Hey! Wait!" he shouted and sprinted forward.

"Boy, yer cuttin' it close. Ya made it just in the nick 'a time, too," the man said as Theo slipped through the crack and into the town. Theo couldn't believe his eyes. Every home in Warren's Hollow was built into the surrounding trees. Many trees had a door at the bottom and windows that went up as far as the eye could see.

"This yer first time in Warren's Hollow, eh?" The man asked.

"How'd you know?" Theo responded

curiously.

"I know that look, son. I've seen it many 'a time."

"Oh," Theo replied as he gazed at the magnificent treehouses. Just as the man turned to walk away, Theo had an idea.

"Wait!" he shouted, and the man turned to face him.

"I'm supposed to be meeting some friends here, but I don't know where they're staying. Could you point me in the right direction?"

"Most travelers stay at River's Edge. Go just straight ahead fer a while, and ya can't miss it. It's on the backside o' town, right next to the river."

"Thank you, mister, uh... Sorry, I guess I didn't catch your name."

"Marty," the man said. He smiled and revealed a row of missing teeth; what few teeth he did have were dark and rotting.

"Thanks. I'm Jirsten," Theo responded. He decided it best to keep his true identity hidden for now.

"See ya around, Jirsten," Marty replied before turning to walk away. Theo headed straight into town, observing both the townspeople and the incredible treehouses along the way. Just as Marty had said, he soon found a tree beside the river with the sign "River's Edge" carved just over the door. Carefully, he opened it and stepped inside.

Theo thought the outside of the trees were impressive until he saw the inside. The diameter of the tree was larger than that of his own home back in Poplar Springs. The tree had been carved hollow on the inside– various tables, chairs, plants, and decorations made the space feel very comfortable. A woman sat behind a counter at the far end of the room.

I need to approach this carefully if I'm going to find them while also keeping our identities a secret, Theo thought as he approached her.

"Hello," Theo said and looked up at her. He tried his best to look innocent and sad.

"What's wrong, sugar?" the woman asked and leaned against the counter.

"Well, I've gotten separated from my friends. I thought they wanted to meet here, but now I'm not sure," Theo said. He lowered his eyes back to the floor and hung his head.

I hope this works.

"Hey, pumpkin," the woman said kindly.

"Maybe I can help. What do your friends look like?"

"Let's see… There are five of them. They are usually wearing long black cloaks," Theo said.

"Oh yes, honey. I do remember seeing some folks like that. They ain't staying here, though," she replied gently as she smiled and wiped the counter down.

"But you saw them? Do you remember where?"

"Yes, I remember. They was leavin' town when I saw them. Seemed to be in a big hurry, too."

"Leaving? You're certain?"

"Yes, sugar. Unless there are other people runnin' 'round here in black cloaks all of a sudden."

"Okay. Thank you, ma'am. You've been very helpful."

"No problem. Hope you find your friends, darlin,'" she replied. Theo quickly backed away and slipped through the door.

Leaving? Why would they be leaving right after they'd arrived? Theo pondered as he walked back toward the gate. He hadn't been walking long when he heard a commotion coming from a nearby treehouse. A crowd of people had gathered and were looking at something, but Theo couldn't quite see what.

Maybe if I can get a little closer, I can see what's happening, he thought.

As he approached, Theo was able to hear individual conversations among the roar of chatter.

"Who are these people?" A man asked.

"I don't know, but we'd better keep a keen eye. The Queen's guard don't play, now. We don't want no part of this."

"Aye. We ought to set watch posts and rotate. If they're here, we'll find 'em."

What are they talking about? Theo thought.

He squeezed his way through the crowd until he was right in front of the treehouse.

Now he understood.

A large *Wanted* sign hung over a poster. On the poster were pictures of each member of Transfigure and, to Theo's dismay, a picture of himself right in the middle. The sign read:

Ye be warned —

Any town caught harboring these fugitives of the crown shall be burnt to the ground by Jhak, the Queen's dragon. These fugitives are considered armed and highly dangerous. If seen, kill on sight. The reward for a body is 10,000 silver coins.

Theo felt all color drain from his face. He was right to keep his identity hidden. Underneath this warning was another note that read:

Important notice —

Theodore Robins is wanted alive. Capture him and be rewarded 50,000 silver coins.

Theo slowly turned and navigated through the crowd, being careful to keep his face down and avoid eye contact.

Only once the crowd was out of sight did he dare to start running. He ran as fast as he could to the city gates. He knew they'd be closed until morning, but he hoped to find another way out of Warren's Hollow; maybe, he thought, he could bribe a guard into letting him slip by if he promised to return with coins. He realized now that Vaymond and the others must have seen the postings and fled the town. He only hoped he could do the same. Finally, in the light of the moon and torches, Theo saw the gate.

Oh no…

It was surrounded by dozens of citizens

of Warren's Hollow. They were armed with pitchforks, torches, and various other household items that Theo couldn't identify. Standing amongst them, to Theo's horror, was Marty.

"Im tellin' ya, he's here. I saw him not long ago. He came in just as the gates were closin'."

"How do you know it was him?" Someone asked from the crowd.

"Trust me! It was him. I talked to him for a time and told him to go to River's End. He said his name was Jirsten."

Knots formed in Theo's stomach. They knew he was here. And at the moment, there didn't appear to be a way out before morning. Even then, the gates would be heavily guarded. Theo knew he'd have to search for another way out of the town.

The river! he thought to himself. *If I can swim across, I'll be free from this town and all of the people in it.*

He decided to avoid the main road at all costs. He wanted to be discreet, but not so much so that he drew unnecessary attention to himself. He traveled this way for quite some time — weaving in and out of treehouses, hiding behind brush piles and wagons or whatever barrier he could find. This way of travel took him much longer, but he found it was necessary in order to avoid the citizens of Warren's Hollow. Finally, he heard the sound of rushing water. He knew the river had to be close by. He continued walking until the tree line came to a stop; beyond that point, there was nothing but an open field between him and the river. And, unfortunately for Theo, dozens of citizens were walking through the clearing. It seemed they knew this was a possible exit point and were taking extra precautions to guard it. The grass between the clearing and the river was roughly knee-high. Theo knew he only had one option.

I'm going to have to crawl and hope that no one sees me.

Theo laid down on his stomach, mustered every ounce of courage he had, and began to crawl forward.

I can do this. I can do this, Theo repeated to himself and continued making his way forward. The river was only a few meters ahead of him now.

"Hey! You! Stop there!" Theo heard someone shout. He froze in his tracks and tried to lay as motionless as possible. He could hear the sound of footsteps approaching.

"Take second guard, will ya? I've gotta take a leak," the voice said.

"Sure thang, Pete," another voice replied. Theo heard the sound of footsteps receding.

Whew! That was close. Okay, just a little further now. I'm going to make it! Theo thought excitedly.

Theo reached the edge of the river and dipped his hand into the flowing water. It was ice cold, but he didn't mind. To him, it felt like freedom. He slowly began crawling, still on his stomach, into the cool river.

A horn blasted to his left.

"Over here! We've got him!" Someone shouted. Just then, dozens of people in the clearing ran toward him. Theo rushed to his feet and dove into the shallow water, submerging himself. The flowing water toppled him end over end, and he struggled to fight against its force. He stayed under until his lungs nearly burst, and his body forced him to come up for a breath. He dove again and repeated the process a few times: swim, come up for air, dive, swim, come up for air, dive. Finally, when he felt he'd covered a good distance, he stayed up for a moment and observed his whereabouts.

"There he is! I see him!" Someone shouted from the riverbank. People were already swimming after him, and he was relieved to find that they were a good distance away. His relief was short-lived when a rope landed just beside him.

"You almost got him, Pete! A little to the left!"

Panicked, he once again continued his routine: swim, come up for air, dive, swim, come up for air, dive. Just as he came up for a breath, he felt a rope tighten around his neck.

"Yeah!"

"You got him!" People on the bank shouted as the rope tugged him backward. He fought against it for a while, but the harder he fought, the tighter its grip became around his neck, and he knew that unless he gave in, he would likely strangle himself. Reluctantly, he let the rope pull him to shore. As he lay on the bank, gasping for breath, someone grabbed his arms and bound them tightly behind his back.

"Thought you'd make it outta here, huh, boy?" He looked up to see Marty's toothless grin smiling down at him.

"We're gonna be rich by sunrise," another voice said.

"The Queen's guards are waitin' for us by the gate. We'll meet 'em there," Marty replied. Theo was forced to his feet. He tried to walk, but his legs gave out from exhaustion, so they dragged him through the clearing.

A loud shriek filled the air. It was a sound Theo immediately recognized.

"What in Vlad's name was *that?*" Marty asked.

"I dunno, Marty. Let's move faster," someone responded.

The shriek sounded again; it was much closer this time. Theo smiled. He looked up to see moonlight glimmering off of ruby-red scales.

Lunell! Luray! Theo thought excitedly. Following closely behind was, Theo assumed, Chauncey; her scales were copper like, the color of amber. She was of similar size to Lunell and Luray, but she had an entirely different appearance. Whereas Lunell and Luray's bodies were thick and stocky, Chauncey's neck was longer and her body leaner, making her appear very agile.

The three landed directly in front of the townspeople. Chauncey released a jet of flames into the air. Dozens of screams sounded as people turned to flee; a few stood frozen in their tracks.

Sitting atop of Luray, black robe rippling in the wind, was Vaymond. Likewise, riding on the back of Lunell was Adoria.

"Release the boy," Adoria warned.

Marty hesitated for a moment. Chauncey growled, and her mouth became bright with flames as she prepared to burn anyone who stood between her and Theodore.

"No! Wait!" Marty cried. He ripped out a pocket knife and cut the ropes that bound Theo's hands. Just then, Theo felt a rush of wind overhead. He looked up to see Rickett encircle the area, and then he landed beside Theo. The townsfolk gaped at the beasts— most had never seen a dragon before, much less four.

Theo approached Rickett and placed his hand on a big claw.

"Thank you," he whispered. Rickett nodded his large head in return.

Theo climbed onto his back, turned to

face the crowd, and then shouted,

"Let it be known!"

The people turned to look at him.

"The Queen is lying to you! She only wants us killed so that all the power in Umbridge is hers for the taking! And with all due respect," —Theo said before spitting on the ground— "Anyone who follows Queen Carmella is a fool and a coward!"

Murmurs of surprise spread throughout the crowd.

"Spread the word!" Theo shouted. He thought of his sister and mother and felt his anger rise like heat from a blazing inferno.

"That I, Theodore Robins, am coming for my sister. And it is not *she* who shall die screaming!" Theo howled in anger and raised a fist to the sky. Rickett spread his wings and raised his head, releasing a jet of flames into the cold night air. Light from the flames reflected in Theo's eyes, revealing a desire that burned within his soul. He was no longer sad. Nor was he afraid.

He was ready.

CHAPTER NINE
TWILIGHT

Theo and the others left Warren's Hollow and landed on a large cliff that rested high upon a nearby mountainside. They rested here for the night, and Theo found comfort in being so high off the ground— no one could possibly reach him, and Queen Carmella wouldn't dare attack five dragons without the full force of her entire army.

"Wake up, Theodore," a gentle voice called.

Theo stretched on the ground where he laid and grudgingly opened his eyes. He found Adoria kneeling over him. She smiled kindly and helped him to his feet.

"Eat some breakfast, Theo. We'll be leaving soon," she insisted as she led him toward a fire where Vaymond was roasting a rabbit on a spit. Lunell, Luray, Chauncey, and Rickett were laying near the edge of a cliff, chewing on the remains of some large animal that was no longer recognizable.

Vaymond offered the rabbit to Theo, which he gratefully accepted. He took a bite and chewed the rabbit slowly, savoring the warm meat's flavor.

"Finish your breakfast," Vaymond announced. The dragons glared at him and returned to their meal.

"We leave for Shru City soon. It will be another long flight, and we need to get there quickly if we are to discover Nelly's whereabouts and enact a plan to rescue her."

"Why are they still in dragon form?" Theo asked.

"Our senses are keener when we are dragons, Theodore. When traveling, usually, at least a few of us are dragons for the entirety of the journey. Dragons can smell a human from miles away, and because each human has a distinct smell, we can also tell how many humans there are. When we are on the lookout for threats, as we are now, that is a very valuable ability."

"I don't understand," Theo frowned. "How can you tell how many humans there are by their individual smells? Wouldn't the smells all blend together?

"Ah, good point. Think of it like this: Say someone is cooking a soup that contains a variety of ingredients. When you are human, all you smell is soup. But when you are a dragon, you smell the onions, the mushrooms, the potatoes, the carrots, the garlic, the broth, the salt, the chiles, all separately. Dragons smell everything this way. Human smells are very different from that of, say, a deer or a bird."

"That makes sense, I guess," Theo replied. "So why aren't you or Adoria in dragon form, then?"

"Because, Theodore, we are the oldest and, therefore, the wisest. As dragons, we cannot speak and, therefore, cannot communicate effectively. We must remain in human form so that we may relay our plans to the others."

"But can't you just change back and forth whenever you want?" Theo asked.

"Well, yes, but it requires a great amount

of energy to transform, and we aren't as young as we once were. It's easier to remain human until we know we must be in dragon form for an extended period of time."

"I see," Theo replied.

Once they'd finished their early morning breakfast, the seven of them set out for Shru City. They flew together for several hours, crossing over the Nebo mountains and over several small towns and villages. They stopped only once so that the dragons could rest their wings, and off they were again. They flew as high as possible to avoid detection from any of the Queen's army. After the events at Warren's Hollow, the Queen knew they were coming. Their only hope now was to form a plan complex enough to rescue Nelly and escape without anyone getting injured or worse. They finally landed around midday in a small clearing a few miles south of Shru City. Vaymond and Adoria instructed the others to remain in the clearing. The plan was this: Vaymond and Adoria would enter the city as spies with the goal of finding Nelly's location and determining the proposed time of sacrifice. Once they had obtained this information, they would return to the clearing, inform the others, and come up with a rescue plan. The only thing Lunell, Luray, Rickett, Chauncey, and Theo had to do was remain undetected.

Vaymond and Adoria left the clearing, leaving Theo alone with the four dragons. The passing minutes felt like hours. Theo paced back and forth through the clearing for a time; he laid on his back and watched the clouds roll by for a time; he talked out loud to the dragons for a time, and they eyed him curiously. Eventually, when the minutes had turned to hours, and the sun was low on the horizon, Theo could take no more.

"That's it. I'm going to find them," he said and jumped to his feet. Chauncey stepped forward and blocked his path. She rumbled with a low growl, and black smoke rose from her nostrils.

"What are you gonna do? Eat me?" Theo challenged.

Chauncey leaned low to the ground in preparation to pounce like a cat on a mouse, and for a moment, Theo wondered if he had made a costly mistake.

Suddenly, Lunell sniffed the air. Chauncey turned to look before sniffing as well.

"Is it them?" Theo asked.

Chauncey nodded.

Sure enough, not long afterward, Vaymond and Adoria came bounding into the clearing.

"Well?" Theo asked. "Did you find anything?"

"We think Nelly is being held inside the temple of Vlad near the backside of the city. Jhak is guarding the temple along with over a thousand warriors. We assume Queen Carmella is there as well," Vaymond stated.

"And the sacrifice? When is it scheduled to take place?" Theo asked impatiently.

"Midnight," Vaymond and Adoria replied in synchronism.

"We heard many rumors," Adoria added.

Midnight? I wonder why... Theo thought to himself. "So what's the plan?"

Vaymond eyed the group cautiously before responding.

"Chauncey and I will attack the temple itself in dragon form. Lunell and Luray will focus on the city gates and ensure that the soldiers outside the city cannot come in. Adoria will remain human. Hopefully, our attacks will cause enough distraction to allow her inside the temple, where she may rescue Nelly and escape the city unnoticed. She will return here with Nelly, where Rickett and you will be waiting. Once Nelly is safe, Rickett will signal us with fire. When we see the signal, we will cease our attacks and retreat together. Then we fly straight to the Stronghold."

"And when do we begin?" asked Theo.

Vaymond looked to see the sun disappear from view, dusking the sky with remnants of twilight.

"Now."

CHAPTER TEN
A PERFECT PLAN

Theo felt a chill rush down his spine. He had known this time would come, but now that it was finally here, a wave of emotions washed over him. The others backed away from Vaymond, giving him plenty of space. They observed quietly as Vaymond began the transformation process– his eyes glowed a soft green, and his body started to emit a greenish light. He shook until his body dispersed into tiny particles, starting with his head and traveling the length of his body until his entire being was now a small cloud that was alive and moving. As the particles multiplied, Vaymond grew. His particles took on a new shape until they finally merged once more, and now, Vaymond was an enormous, dark green dragon. His mighty shoulders and legs rippled with muscles as he stretched, no doubt getting comfortable in his new body. On top of his nose was a large horn that curved upward and slightly back.

Perfect for tearing flesh, Theo thought to himself.

Vaymond was at least twice the size of the other dragons, if not more. He still, however, was not as immense as Jhak. With Chauncey's agility and swiftness and Vaymond's brute power and strength, Theo was sure they would prove to be formidable foes.

Vaymond spread his wings in preparation for flight. He lept into the air- the force of his powerful legs making the ground shake and causing Theo to lose his balance. His wings seemed to strain as they fought to lift his large body. Chauncey followed after him, gracefully leaping into the air with ease. She rolled her body, spun, and shot forward like a torpedo. Theo smiled.

Show off.

Lunell and Luray were next. They each took a running start and jumped, climbing into the sky and taking a slightly different direction, no doubt heading for the city gates. Adoria bounded into the woods, leaving Theo and Rickett alone.

Theo began to pace, unable to sit still with the amount of adrenaline pumping through his body. His heart pounded rapidly in his chest as he walked about the clearing.

Theo heard distant screaming and stopped to listen. Several loud shrieks sounded in the distance, followed by loud explosions. He assumed this must be Lunell and Luray torching the gates and the warriors outside the city. He imagined Vaymond and Chauncey fighting both a thousand warriors and Jhak. He shuddered at the thought.

How will Adoria ever make it to the temple?

"Rickett, we have to help," Theo said. He looked up at Rickett's soft blue eyes.

Rickett shook his large head.

"We have to, Rickett! They can't do this without us!"

Rickett sat firmly on the ground, a sign that he had no intention of leaving.

"If they can't get Adoria into that temple, then my sister is going to be burned alive by *your* father!" Theo screamed. Rickett stared at Theo for a moment and then hung his head in shame. Theo immediately wished he could take back those words.

"Look, Rickett, I didn't mean it. I'm sorry," Theo consoled. "I only want to help, that's all. I know it's not your fault that Jhak is your father. You are a good person, Rickett."

Rickett continued to hang his head.

"Listen to me, Rickett. Please," Theo said as he walked forward and placed a hand on Rickett's large claw. Rickett peered down at him with sad eyes.

"Hey, listen. I know what I said was mean and stupid, and I hope you can forgive me for that. But I do know this– you have been here for me, even when you didn't have to. You took me to Warren's Hollow, and you're here now. I know you may feel guilty that Jhak betrayed Transfigure and killed my father, and maybe that's why you've seemed so reluctant to speak to me since I arrived at the Stronghold, but Rickett, I don't blame you for it. The actions of your father have nothing, absolutely nothing, to do with you or who you are as a person. You are kind, gentle, and selfless. That I can already see."

Rickett looked up at him now, and Theo could see the surprise flash in his eyes.

"I mean it, Rickett. You are good. You aren't like him."

Rickett lifted his head.

"And you don't owe me anything. You don't have to help me save my sister– that choice is yours and yours alone to make. But I do ask you, as my friend, will you help me?"

Rickett shrieked and lowered himself to the ground, allowing Theo to climb up.

"Yeah!" Theo shouted excitedly. He jumped up, grabbed one of Rickett's neck spikes, and swung himself onto his back. "Let's go find Adoria!"

Rickett leapt into the air and flew upwards. Shru City came into view within seconds as Rickett carried them into the sky. Theo saw black smoke coming from the city gates and saw Lunell perched atop them. Luray was in front of the city, torching the Queen's soldiers.

If Vaymond catches a glimpse of us, the distraction could be all it takes for Jhak to gain the upper hand.

Rickett must have had the same thought because, to Theo's relief, he carried them higher and higher until they were above the clouds, using them as cover to avoid detection.

"We have to find Adoria!" Theo shouted over the wind. Rickett nodded his large head in acknowledgement.

How will we find her in all of this mess? It seems impossible! Unless…

"Rickett! Can you smell her?"

Rickett lifted his head into the air and closed his eyes for concentration. He sniffed a few times and then looked back and shook his head.

Ugh! The wind must be blowing her smell away from us, Theo concluded.

Theo thought for a moment before shouting, "We know she's headed for the temple! Let's circle the city and approach from the backside! They won't be expecting us from that direction! Then we'll land and search for her on the ground!"

Rickett launched forward as he began to circle the city's western edge, being careful to use the clouds as a barrier whenever possible.

Where are Vaymond and Chauncey? We

should have seen them by now.

Almost as if in response to his thoughts, Theo heard an explosion from above. He looked up just in time to see a bright light flash and then disappear.

They're fighting from above! They must have lured Jhak away from the temple, Theo thought.

Once Rickett had circled the city, he approached the backside of the temple and hovered over the cover of a cloud. He looked back at Theo.

"I'm ready! Let's go!" he shouted.

Rickett folded his wings and nosedived.

"Aghhhhhhhh!" Theo screamed as he held tightly to Rickett's neck spike. Rickett fanned out his wings just as they neared the ground and landed with a soft thump.

People screamed in fright at the sight of Rickett. Theo ignored them.

Theo heard another explosion from above. He looked up in time to see the silhouette of a dragon through the clouds. He shivered.

Somewhere, a person screamed.

"What about now, Rickett? Can you smell her?"

Rickett raised his head once more and

inhaled deeply. He then lurched forward and ran to the temple's left side.

That must be a yes! Theo thought excitedly.

Rickett continued running until they came upon a group of ten soldiers. The soldiers had encircled Adoria and were slowly closing in on her. Adoria was covered in blood, and her lips were curled in a snarl. She was gripping the hilt of a long sword and swung ferociously at any soldier who stepped forward.

Rickett approached the group and roared loudly in an attempt to frighten the soldiers away. Three fled, but seven remained. Adoria used this distraction to attack the soldier closest to her, jutting her sword through his chest.

Rickett swiped one soldier with his claw, sending him flying twenty yards away; his body crumpled awkwardly to the ground, where he then lay motionless. Four soldiers remained now as another turned and fled.

Adoria attacked another soldier, a large man with a broad chest and a battle ax. Although he outsized her, his armor weighed him down, and his movements were slow. Adoria dodged his swinging ax with ease, sliding between his legs, turning, and piercing her sword through his back. He fell to his knees before face-planting into the ground.

Three soldiers remained.

The soldiers faced Rickett, jabbing spears at his chest. Rickett released a stream of fire onto the soldiers, who screamed and ran about frantically as their bodies went up in flames.

"You could've just done that to begin with!" Theo exclaimed.

Theo made eye contact with Adoria, and she smiled at him gratefully. Her smile soon disappeared, though, when an arrow came flying from above and sank right into her side. She gasped and fell. Rickett shrieked and caught her with a large paw just before she hit the ground. Rickett roared ferociously at the archer who sat atop the temple's roof. The archer climbed the temple roof in an effort to escape. Rickett, who was mad with rage, jumped up, still holding Adoria in his claw, and with a few flaps of his wings, landed directly in front of the man. The man could only stare with wide eyes as Rickett sank his teeth into his skull and shook him violently before throwing him over the roof's edge. Theo quickly climbed down and ran over to Adoria.

"Adoria!" He exclaimed as he took her face in his hands.

"Theo," she whispered weakly.

"Just hold on, Adoria. We're gonna get you out of here," he said, tears rolling down his cheeks.

"Save your sister," she said and grabbed Theo's hand.

"I can't leave you here," he sobbed.

"Go, Theo. You must."

Theo nodded and looked up at Rickett.

"Stay with her. Keep her safe," he said. "But first, do you think you can help me inside?"

Rickett stomped with one paw until his foot broke through the roof, leaving a hole just large enough for Theo's body. Theo peered inside.

"It's too far down, Rickett. I need you to make it larger and hoist me down with your tail."

Rickett continued stomping until more of the hole's outer edge broke free. Rickett dangled his tail into the hole. Theo carefully grabbed onto one of his spikes.

"Okay, Rickett. Now!" Theo shouted.

Rickett lowered his tail down until Theo

was on the ground.

"Wait there!" Theo shouted. "I'll call for you when I'm ready!"

Rickett grunted in affirmation.

Theo took a moment to observe his surroundings. He appeared to be in the temple's main chamber. The room was large and filled with long rows of benches for the people who attended religious services. At the back of the room was a large statue of Vlad, the God of Power. Most Umbrigdians worshiped all five Gods; Vlad, however, was the pinnacle of worship. The other four Gods– Rona, Clain, Nidern, and Sophoria, were all said to have been appointed by Vlad himself. He was the source of all power in the universe, and the other four Gods were but a vessel to *his* spiritual realm.

The statue was immense— it rose from the floor to the ceiling. It displayed Vlad as a large, bald man dressed in armor and wearing a cape that rippled to the floor. Theo admired the craftsmanship.

It's incredible that something made of stone could appear to ripple like water, he thought.

"Hello," an elegant voice suddenly called from behind. Theo recognized it immediately.

He turned to find Queen Carmella standing a few yards away from him, smiling devilishly. "We've been waiting for you, *Theodore* Robins," her smooth voice called.

She sidestepped, and behind her, bound and badly beaten, was Nelly.

CHAPTER ELEVEN
THE GREAT ESCAPE

"Nelly!" Theo cried.

Nelly slowly lifted her head.

"Theodore," she whispered. Her cheeks were sunken, and her eyes dark and bruised. It didn't seem that she had eaten since her capture three days prior. To Theo, it felt like he hadn't seen her in a lifetime.

"What have you done to her?!" Theo yelled with rage.

Queen Carmella laughed.

"Your sister's looks won't matter in a few hours, *Theodore*. Not once Vlad receives this *precious* offering," Queen Carmella said as she tenderly brushed the hair from Nelly's face.

"Don't touch her!" Theo screamed. He charged forward, ready to end the Queen with his bare hands if he must.

"Guards," the Queen stated calmly. Five guards poured into the room and grabbed Theo by the arms. He frantically struggled to free himself.

The Queen walked forward and bent down until she was at eye level with him.

"Let me fill you in on a little secret, *Theodore*," the Queen whispered. "I know of your family *secret*. I know that either you or your sister has dragon's blood pumping through your veins. I don't know if it's your sister or you who is the dragon, which is why, since you're here now, I'll offer you *both* to Vlad." The Queen placed her cold hand on his cheek. Theo struggled to move away, but the guards held him still.

"Oh, Theodore, how you favor your father," she smiled. Theo stopped squirming.

"What? You didn't know? Oh," she clicked her tongue, "that's a shame. Yes, I met your father once in the Battle of Narwhal Bay. He burned a good number of my ships and my men. He transformed, turning human before me, and begged that I show mercy for the people of Bulmar. He knew I could not be defeated. I declined the offer, which he was not very happy about. He could have killed me then and there, but he didn't. He had a very gentle heart. He just quickly transformed again and *flew* away. Looking back, I realize he was only trying to protect you and your *sweet* sister. It was very touching." The Queen poked out her bottom lip. "Little did he know, Jhak had already come to me that night. He'd flown out to meet me long before we reached shore. He told me of the curse and the other dragons and made a proposal."

Theo listened with horror.

"He said that he would take out your leader, his own brother, if he could join me in conquering Umbridge. You see, *Jhak* and I are very like-minded individuals. Of course, I saw the potential in having a dragon by my side, so I accepted. Jhak killed your father that night... on *my* orders," she giggled. "Just like he's going to kill Nelly and then your mother and all of your other little *Transfigure* friends."

Theo screamed with rage. The Queen smiled.

"Poor, poor Theodore. Don't worry, I'll make sure he kills you *last.*"

Queen Carmella stood and walked away from him as she continued talking.

"You see, I've been waiting quite some time for this opportunity. Vaymond has grown old and weak, and you and your sister are old enough to kill without so much as a peep from the people of Umbridge. Had I killed you as toddlers, well, that would have caused an uproar. But now that you're older, I can kill you both and call it a *sacrifice,* and no one will so much as bat an eye. Without the threat of you or your sister and Vaymond out of the picture, well, I know that taking out the others will be as simple as plucking daisies from a roadside ditch."

A loud crash sounded from overhead. The Queen looked up and squinted her eyebrows.

"Guards, take Theodore and Nelly elsewhere. And summon Jhak to quickly finish those two. It's nearly time."

The crashing sounds continued as a guard responded, "Yes, Queen."

Just then, part of the ceiling crumbled, sending large chunks of stone onto the floor around them. Rickett's large head entered the room. He roared ferociously, causing the Queen and her guards to shield their ears.

"Take them! Now!" She shouted.

The guards lifted Nelly off the ground and began to carry her away, dragging Theo behind. Rickett viciously clawed at the ceiling, breaking pieces away as he tried to make room for the rest of his body.

"Rickett!" Theo called. Rickett roared again and applied all his strength to the final chunk of the ceiling. He came crashing into the room. The guards quickened their pace. Rickett jumped, glided over them, and blocked their path.

Rickett stood snarling, black smoke billowing from his nostrils and breathing heavily. His eyes were slanted, his head poised high, and his chest puffed out. The sight sent shivers down Theo's spine.

Queen Carmella whispered, "Let them go," and quietly backed away. The guards dropped Nelly and released their grip on Theo. They followed her until Queen Carmella came to a door. She slipped out quickly, with her guards right on her tail.

Theo ran to Nelly.

"Nell," he sobbed.

"Theo," she whispered faintly and touched his cheek with a trembling hand.

"Let's get her out of here, Rickett," Theo said.

Rickett carefully wrapped one giant claw around Nelly's body. Theo climbed onto his back, and Rickett jumped through the hole in the ceiling and back onto the roof. Adoria was there waiting, her breath slow and labored.

"Can you carry all three of us, Rickett?" Theo asked. Rickett, as if in response, reached out his other front claw and delicately wrapped it around Adoria. Then, using his hind legs, he kicked and carried them into the air. Theo could sense the strain in Rickett's muscles as he struggled to carry the extra weight. He flew toward Lunell and Luray at the city gates and found them perched on the walls. Lunell saw them first and jumped down to meet them. She sniffed Adoria and whimpered softly. She then looked over at Nelly, and Theo could see the surprise in her eyes.

"Lunell, can you carry Adoria?" Theo asked.

Rickett transferred Adoria into Lunell's claws. Lunell nuzzled Adoria gently.

Luray glided down to join them.

"Luray, my sister is too weak to ride. Will you carry her?"

Luray nodded and took Nelly in his talons.

"Let's go!" Theo shouted. "We light the signal, wait for Vaymond and Chauncey, and fly together to the Stronghold!"

With that, the three of them took flight. It wasn't long before they reached the clearing. They hovered side by side and joined together a stream of flames that reached high into the sky. They went on like this until the heat from the fire was nearly too much for Theo to bear. Finally, they stopped.

"Did they see it?" Theo queried. He knew they couldn't respond, but he was too anxious to remain silent. Sure enough, before long, Theo could make out the shape of a large dragon descending from the clouds. His eyes anxiously searched until, finally, he saw Chauncey following close behind.

He sighed in relief.

Theo halfway expected to see Jhak flying

close on their tail, but to his surprise, he wasn't. Jhak was still unaware of Nelly's rescue, and he probably assumed that Vaymond and Chauncey had given up and were retreating. Vaymond and Chauncey joined them, and, never landing, they flew as fast as they could away from Shru City.

CHAPTER TWELVE
NOW WE WAIT

The five dragons flew for six hours. They passed Warren's Hollow and flew deep into the heart of the Nebo mountains before they dared to stop and rest. They veered toward a cave that was large enough to fit every dragon except for Vaymond. Vaymond landed first, followed by Luray. The others hovered in the air. With a flash of green light, Vaymond was human again. He walked into the cave, and the others quickly followed.

Theo jumped down from Rickett's back and immediately rushed to Nelly, who Luray had gently laid on the ground.

"Nelly! Are you okay?" Theo asked.

"Water," she whispered through parched lips.

Theo ran to Luray, who was carrying saddlebags filled with necessities they had brought on their journey. He quickly removed a canteen of water and rushed back to Nelly.

"Here," he said as he helped her lift her head. With shaking hands, she grabbed the container and took many big gulps. Theo heard footsteps and looked up to see Vaymond, garbed in his long, black cloak, approaching them.

"Nelly," he said, bending down. "It is nice to finally meet you."

Nelly eyed him questioningly. "You are the green dragon," she stated weakly.

"That I am, Nelly, that I am," he smiled.

Adoria!

"Vaymond! Adoria is badly wounded! We have to help her!" Theo shouted.

Lunell had not long since landed and released Adoria from her grasp. Adoria was lying motionless on the ground. Vaymond and Theo approached her. Theo watched as Vaymond ripped the bottom portion of her shirt, exposing the arrow in her body. Adoria was sweating profusely.

"The arrow must be removed and the area cauterized," Vaymond said. "That is all we can do to help her." He grabbed the arrowhead. "Hold her still, Theodore."

Theo sat cross-legged and placed Adoria's head in his lap. She was still unconscious.

"On three, Theodore, I'm going to snap this arrowhead off and pull the shaft out from the other side. Once I snap off the tip, I need your help rolling her on her side so I can pull the rest of it out."

"Okay," he huffed.

Vaymond handed him a cloth. "It's going to bleed," he said. "A lot."

Theo grabbed the cloth and squeezed until his knuckles turned white.

"Breathe, Theodore. I need you to be strong," Vaymond said.

Theo tried his best to relax.

Vaymond removed Adoria's sword from its sheath and glanced up at Lunell, who was standing over them.

"Lunell, when I give the signal, I need you to heat the tip of Adoria's sword."

Lunell nodded.

Vaymond looked at Theodore now. "Are

you ready?"

"Yes," Theo replied.

"Okay. One, two, three!" he shouted and then broke off the tip of the arrow. Adoria stirred slightly and groaned.

Theo helped Vaymond roll her on her side.

"Remember, Theodore. It's going to bleed," he said.

"I remember," Theo assured him.

Slowly, Vaymond pulled the arrow out of Adoria's body. She groaned loudly.

Just as Vaymond had said, when the arrow was removed, it began gushing blood. Theo held a cloth to each side and pushed down, holding it tightly.

Vaymond held up the sword. "Now, Lunell!"

Lunell released a stream of fire onto the sword until its tip glowed a bright red.

"Hold her, Theodore," Vaymond said.

He pressed the tip of the hot sword onto the site of the wound. Adoria screamed.

"Shhhhhh, Adoria. It's okay. It'll be over soon," Theo coaxed.

"Now we must do the other side,"

Vaymond said. Theo nodded.

Once again, he pressed down onto the wound in her back where the arrow had entered her body. Adoria screamed again, sending chills down Theo's spine. She continued to whimper for a while and fell silent once more.

"Now what?" Theo asked.

"Now we wait," Vaymond replied.

So they did. They waited for the remainder of that evening and into the night. Theo attempted to sleep, but thoughts of Adoria kept him awake. He tossed and turned. He paced. He threw rocks over the mountain's edge. Finally, when he'd nearly given up hope, Vaymond came to him.

"Come, Theodore. She's awake."

Theo followed Vaymond into the cave where Adoria lay against Lunell. She smiled weakly when she saw Theo. Nelly was beside her as well.

"Adoria!" Theo exclaimed and ran to her side. "I was so worried."

"I am proud of you, Theo. Without your help and your bravery, I would have surely died fighting those soldiers. And we would not be here together now, with Nelly."

Tears formed in the corner of Theo's eyes, and a single tear rolled down his cheek.

"She wouldn't be here if not for you," Theo sniffed. "Or you," Theo said as he looked up at Rickett. He had been silently watching from a distance.

"Or Rickett," Adoria agreed.

Vaymond stood over them with his arms crossed.

"While you may have saved your sister," he said to both Rickett and Theo, "you directly defied my orders. Not once, but twice now. It was reckless and impulsive. You could've gotten yourselves killed. You could've gotten Nelly killed. You could've gotten us all killed." Theo and Rickett lowered their eyes, avoiding Vaymond's gaze.

"But," Vaymond said, "you didn't."

Both Theo and Rickett exchanged surprised glances.

"While you may have been reckless and impulsive," Vaymond continued, "you were also brave."

Theo looked at Vaymond.

"Had it not been for your cunningness and strength, Adoria and Nelly would surely be dead. Your father would be proud," Vaymond boasted. "As am I."

Theo tried to stop the tears, but they continued to fall from his face uncontrollably.

"Thank you," he sobbed.

Vaymond smiled. "Try and get some rest now," he said to Theo and the others. "We cannot stay here long. We leave first thing in the morning, straight for the Stronghold."

CHAPTER THIRTEEN
THE BLOOD DRAGON CURSE

They awoke early the next morning and began the long flight back to the Stronghold. They flew for many hours and stopped only twice to rest. At last, Mount Dyer came into view. Theo smiled with relief at the sight of the waterfall. They flew into the mouth of the cave, and their bodies crumpled to the floor with exhaustion. After resting for some time, everyone transformed back into humans and garbed themselves with their black cloaks. Vaymond assured Theo that although Adoria had a close brush with death, she would be just fine. Nelly was back to herself within a couple of days. She ate, rested, and visited with the others. She enjoyed the epic tale of Theo's escape from the dungeon and his run-in with Transfigure, who, to her surprise, were their family. But not just any family, a family of dragons.

A week after Nelly's rescue, Vaymond invited everyone to the Great Hall, as Theo learned it was called, for a feast. Spirits were high as Adoria joined them for the first time since their return. When the feast was over, Vaymond said, "Theodore, Nelly. You know of Jaxton Robins and of the Blood Dragon Curse. However..." Vaymond paused as his face grew serious, "I have not been entirely honest with you."

Theo's eyes grew wide with surprise. "What do you mean?" he asked.

"There is another reason why we call our... *condition* the Blood Dragon Curse. It was found long ago by your grandfather, Tayvior Robins, that if a person possesses the dragon enzyme causing them to transform, the enzyme can be triggered by coming into contact with an *active* enzyme."

Theo scrunched his eyebrows together with confusion. "That doesn't make any sense. But—I mean how—" he scratched his head.

"Aren't enzymes found in your blood?"

"Aye. That's right."

"Wait a minute, are you saying that–"

"That you can drink dragon's blood and transform if you are a Shaker. Yes, Theodore. That's what I'm saying."

"Drinking dragon's blood will bring on the immediate onset of transformation," Nelly interrupted. She was looking at Vaymond intently now.

"Correct," Vaymond smiled.

"So if Nelly and I drink dragon's blood…"

"Then whichever of you is the dragon will immediately transform," Vaymond confirmed.

A cold chill went through Theo's body at the thought of turning into a dragon, as he had seen happen so many times now.

"If we are to save our mother," Nelly stated, "then we need all the help we can get. We will be of more use if we can transform as well."

"Correct again," Vaymond replied.

"I don't know…" Theo mumbled.

"Theo, you must be brave. Ma needs us," Nelly encouraged. "We must do this."

Theo hesitated and then, half-heartedly,

agreed.

Vaymond led the two of them away from the table and to the other side of the room, where he had already set out two cups and a long, slender knife in preparation for this occasion. Theo gulped.

Vaymond grabbed the knife and, very carefully, sliced the palm of his hand. He squeezed a small stream of blood into one cup and then the other.

"You're sure this will work?" Theo asked nervously.

"I'm sure," Vaymond replied.

Lunell, Luray, Adoria, Chauncey, and Rickett gathered around now.

"It's okay, Theo," Lunell urged. Theo looked at Rickett, who nodded his head in approval.

With trembling hands, Theo reached forward and grabbed the chalice. The metal felt cold in his hand. Sweat beads formed on his forehead.

Nelly reached out and lifted her cup as well.

"For Ma," she said.

"For Ma," he agreed.

Slowly, he lifted the cup to his lips. The blood was warm and thick, nearly making him gag. He tried to ignore the taste.

Still trembling, Theo lowered the cup back to the table.

"I-I- don't feel any different," he stammered. "How long will this take?"

"It has already begun," Nelly chimed.

Theo looked at Nelly to see her eyes, calm and tranquil as ever, glowing with a soft, white light.

Lindsey Camber, age twenty-seven, was born and raised in rural West Tennessee. Her love for reading began at the age of ten, when she fell in love with fantasy, especially when the stories had anything to do with dragons. After graduating high school, Lindsey obtained her Bachelors in Communication at the University of Memphis and her Masters in Education at Western Governors University. Now an singer-songwriter in her hometown, Lindsey enjoys writing in her free time. Lindsey mostly loves writing about ferocious beasts, such as dragons and other monsters, that make her readers' hair stand on end.